LUSTY LETTERS

MISTRESS IN THE MAKING, BOOK TWO

LARISSA LYONS

Lusty Letters is dedicated to Christina. Thank you for the hours of laughs (and bawdy conversations I've not had with anyone *outside my characters' heads* ☺*). You lift my heart; so delighted, am I, to have found a similar risqué sense of humor and such a wondrous friend. Now, girl, just when are we going to get matching tattoos?* >^..^<

This series is dedicated to anyone who has difficulty speaking up for themselves. May you find a way to be heard.

Lusty Letters Copyright © 2020 by Larissa Lyons
Published by Literary Madness

ISBN 978-1-949426-18-2 (Paperback)
ISBN 978-1-949426-17-5 (E-book)

Proofread by Judy Zweifel at Judy's Proofreading; Copy edits by ELF at elewkf1@yahoo.com; Edited by Elizabeth St. John; Cover by Victoria Cooper

At Literary Madness, we strive to create a book free of typos. If you notice anything amiss, we're happy to fix it. litmadness@yahoo.com

CONTENTS

LUSTY LETTERS

LUSTY LETTERS

A note...speaking peace and tenderness in every line.

— JANE AUSTEN, *NORTHANGER ABBEY*

WHEREUPON THINGS PROGRESS
NICELY – AND NAUGHTILY

Get posts and letters, and make friends with speed.

William Shakespeare, *King Henry IV*

———————◗◖———————

THE FIRST ATTEMPT (the strip of paper it was on cut away, now balled up and swept to the floor):

Mrs. Hurwell–

What a horrid beginning. Did he *want* to instill more distance between them?

Second attempt:

Thea,

Please accept my most humble thanks—

"Humble thanks?" *What am I? Her deuced hat maker?*

Fourth attempt (currently being batted about by Cyclops, along with the other three):

Thea,

I count the hours until next we meet—

"Ballocks!" He wasn't ready to pen poetical-sounding odes to her either.

"Woof!" Cyclops agreed as yet another piece of crumpled paper was relegated to the empty grate.

Seventh (and final) attempt:

Thea,

Thank you for an enjoyable evening. I recalled someone mentioning you have a particular fondness for Byron. In all honesty, I cannot tolerate poetry (his or any others') so please accept this volume with my sincere wish that it brings you pleasure.

Until tonight, Tremayne

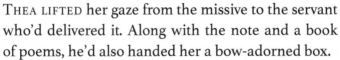

THEA LIFTED her gaze from the missive to the servant who'd delivered it. Along with the note and a book of poems, he'd also handed her a bow-adorned box.

The spry young man had introduced himself as,

"Buttons, miss, since I was caught eatin' one, with loads of others found missing. My papa told me once that our ma despaired but I don't remember, on account of being jus' months old at the time."

"What is etiquette in this regard?" she asked, smiling at the informative Buttons and gesturing toward the gifts and letter she now held. Thea hoped he knew—for she surely didn't. "Is Lord Tremayne expecting a reply?"

Not quite twenty, the youth was broad as a barn and twice as sturdy. His blunt-featured face was turned charming by the decisive cowlick that flipped up a good portion of his sandy-brown hair on the left side of his forehead. He'd told her, when he swiped the offending cowlick for the third time, that he had a twin, one whose hair misbehaved on the opposite side. "Expectin'? A reply?" He pondered a moment. "That I cannot say certain-like, but I do be thinkin' he might be hopin' fer one."

"Oh?"

"Aye." The young man dressed in formal livery stepped forward from his perch on the small landing just outside her townhouse. He tilted his head toward her ear, as though about to impart a confidence he didn't want her hovering new butler to overhear. "I was told to take my time in returnin'."

Assuming the ornate desk in the sumptuous drawing room was as well supplied as the rest of the residence, Thea was confident her eager fingers would have no trouble locating paper and ink.

"Would you mind waiting in the kitchen while I compose one?"

She'd met the married couple hired to serve as caretakers and knew Mrs. Samuels was downstairs baking this very moment.

With a glance at Mr. Samuels, who had summoned Thea to the door once informed Lord Tremayne had requested his servant place the missive directly into her keeping, the spiffy footman stepped back a pace and diffidently crossed his arms behind his back, giving her a casual shake of his head. "I'll jus' wait here, ma'am. Take what time you need."

"Outside?" When intermittent rains thundered down for the second day in a row, making the uncovered porch damp and dreary? "Poppycock!"

A quick look at Mr. Samuels—and the nod he gave her—confirmed Thea's intuition, and she tugged the visiting servant over the threshold by one sleeve and pointed. "The kitchen is tucked at the back of that hallway, down the single flight of stairs. Mind you ask Mrs. Samuels to let you sample her lemon tarts."

When the young man smiled wider than the Thames, Thea suspected he had a fondness for baked goods. Either that or he'd caught sight of the painted nudes.

His next words illustrated how very wrong she was. "I'm right glad he found you, miss."

．　．　．

HE BEING LORD TREMAYNE?

Well, of course. Who else could the footman mean? But to be told so directly—that a servant was glad his master had "found" *her*?

It was...unexpected, unusual.

It was flattering to the point that flutters abounded in her belly as Thea situated herself at the angled writing desk. She used the familiar task of readying the quill as she contemplated just what to say.

How did one answer the first note from their new protector? (Dare she hope it was the first of several?)

More importantly, how did she respond to the man who'd spent his seed on her back in the most intimate of acts but who hadn't spoken more than a paragraph to her all evening? And a paltry paragraph at that.

"Just reply to him as he addresses you," the words were out before she'd thought them through, echoing a semblance of Sarah's previous advice. "Same tone, same length."

Aye, that should suffice.

THIRTY MINUTES LATER, a significant portion of which she'd wasted staring at the blank sheet, Thea had finally managed to fill it in, not quite to capacity but close. She wafted the page through the air, encouraging the ink to dry.

Lord Tremayne,

I delight in finding common ground, for despite public opinion to the contrary, I do not find much to appreciate in Byron. Based on the works I've read, he's overly dramatic for my tastes. Robert Burns, now, I adore and admit to a frisson (a small one, I assure you) of dismay at learning you hold no particular fondness for poetry. None at all? Are you quite certain? (I must clarify, you see, as it is something I find nearly incomprehensible.)

As to the volume you sent, I will treasure it always (are not gifts meant to be treasured?) though I will admit I am already in possession of this particular volume—and through no purchase of my own. I come to think mayhap Hatchards put it on sale?

Please, I beseech you, read the next few lines with your mind unfettered by past opinions:

> *Wee, sleekit, cow'rin, tim'rous beastie,*
> *O, what a panic's in thy breastie!*
> *Thou need na start awa sae hasty,*
> *Wi' bickering brattle!*
> *I wad be laith to rin an' chase thee,*
> *Wi' murd'ring pattle!*

Do these lines not speak to you? Are you not curious to know more? To learn the fate of this dear, wee beastie?

What of the incomparable Mr. William Shakespeare? Do you find anything in his work recommends itself to you? Oh, dear. I believe this must be a magical quill I employ

for it has quite run away with my tongue. Do forgive me.
(But here, I must interject: this new home I find myself
situated in feels magical indeed. It is lovely. More serene
than anywhere I've lived before. I do thank you, most
sincerely. And will endeavor to please you in exchange.)

I anticipate tonight with a smile.

Dor Thea

"Same tone, same *length*?" Bah. Brevity had never been one of her particular talents.

Frowning at herself, Thea folded the paper and sealed it with wax and the generic stamp she'd found in the desk. "You'd better hope that during the reading of it he doesn't nod off."

———————◦———————

Daniel laughed and laughed again.

The demure little chit had taken him to task! That would teach him to deride all poetry in one unwarranted swoop.

And serene? She found that garish abode *serene*?

Another chuckle escaped.

He checked his pocket watch. It was scarce after 2:00 p.m. Hours yet until dark. Hours yet until he could feast his starved eyes on her again and see whether she was truly as lovely as he recalled.

"Rum fogged, I am," he muttered, reaching for another sheet.

Ah. I see now.

Like a pokered-up prig of a tutor, you've decided I shall admire poetic lines or else? Is that it?

As to the verses you so, ah, eloquently shared, might I put forth a request for future examples to be in <u>English</u>? My beastie-gibberish has fair run amok, you see. And the longer I attempt to decipher what causes your wee beastie's breastie to panic, I fear my own crown office has been split asunder by a "murd'ring pattle" (what, pray, is a pattle, murdering or otherwise?).

No doubt, now you'll be regretting the bargain we've made, your fair, <u>fine</u> breastie in a bickering brattle (though what the deuce that is, I haven't a clue) over your benefactor's lack of appreciation for lyrical, metrical prose. What can I do to redeem myself in your eyes?

Aha! Inspiration strikes...

He jumped up to scrounge his library. After a thorough search, he retrieved several leather-bound volumes from one of the topmost shelves. Volumes that sent dust motes dancing in the air when he dared blow on them. Volumes that protested when he opened the aged spines for the first time since inheriting the London house along with the title but that practically sang to him when he started reading...and searching...

Mayhap I should illustrate my tastes in poetic literature? If nothing else to set your concern to rest.

To borrow a bit from the glorious Bard himself...

> *HAMLET: Lady, shall I lie in your lap?*

> *OPHELIA: No, my lord.*

> *HAMLET: I mean, my head upon your lap?*

> *OPHELIA: Ay, my lord.*

> *HAMLET: Do you think I meant country matters?*

> *OPHELIA: I think nothing, my lord.*

> *HAMLET: That's a fair thought to lie between maids' legs.*

> *OPHELIA: What is, my lord?*

> *HAMLET: Nothing.*

> *OPHELIA: You are merry, my lord.*

Me? A merry lord? I confess it's not something I've ever thought of myself—until just this moment. Perhaps it is your poetical prompting that makes it so.

Ergo, as I inappropriately must point out (or could it be considered <u>appropriate</u>, given the intimacies inherent in our liaison?), where it concerns country matters pertaining to the beautiful female of my recent acquaintance, I find much to admire in Shakespeare. As I find much to admire in her (You, should you be at all unclear).

Pity the verses I tend to admire are not of the socially acceptable variety. Therefore I shall endeavor to find something more proper:

> *Shall I compare thee to a summer's day?*
> *Thou art more lovely and more temperate...*

"Shall I compare thee to a summer's day?" Oh, how could you try to bamboozle me with that one?

I doubt anyone with half a modicum of any brain matter at all would be unable to pull that out of their hat. But you do earn points for entertainment (if not for effort). And I must commend your penmanship as well. It's bold and sprawling (much like I surmise your shoulders and chest would appear sans shirt if I were given to considering such a thing).

"Dorothea Jane, should you be so vulgar? Hinting that you want to see his chest..."

Hinting? You came right out and wrote it!

"And blast me to Bedfordshire and back if I'm

not about to leave it!" With a hearty (and unfamiliar) feeling of burgeoning confidence, she continued...

After all, he'd started it.

And though I should be shamed to admit it to anyone save you, I find your inappropriate, illicit Shakespeare much to my liking. The thought of your head upon my lap sounds lovely indeed. Have you a picnic in mind? Gazing overhead at the clouds as they skitter past?

Or perhaps you have something more earthy in mind?

I—

Thea's quill leapt from the page as though blasted backward from the mouth of a musket. "Nay, I cannot write that."

She couldn't. Shouldn't. It was wicked. Wanton beyond measure. But oh, how the naughty thought tempted...

Follow his lead.

Thea reasoned, given the sage advice Sarah had imparted, she could really do no less. After all, if she couldn't be boldly flirty with him in person, then why not indulge the urge now, when he'd been the one to include the erotic wordplay?

Determinedly, Thea re-inked the tip and continued.

I confess, upon first reading, my eyes skimmed your letter so quickly they fairly skipped over part of Hamlet and

Ophelia's exchange. Imagine my astonishment when I thought I read of your <u>head</u> lying between my legs. (Forgive me! I most ardently intended to write <u>his</u> head, his— Hamlet's—between a maiden's le— Oh, bother it!)

Face flaming, Thea lifted the quill and watched her shaking hand hover above the page.

She should cross it out. The entire last paragraph. It was completely beyond the pale.

Nay. She should trim the page and start anew.

She looked at the thick stack of fresh paper, then back at the sheet before her, only half filled in.

Starting anew would be very wasteful. And had Thea not learned economies, in every aspect of her life, the past few months?

Tell yourself the truth, girl. It wasn't thrift that had her continuing on the same page. It was the tingling awareness Lord Tremayne's presence had brought to her body last night. The awareness that had only grown in hours since he'd left...

You see in me a pokered-up prig of a tutor? My lord, how you wound me with such a comparison. Could you not think of me more along the lines of a spruced-up sprite of a governess? Or a buttoned-up— (Fiddletwig! I must cry off here. I cannot think of any suitable, single-syllable B-word that might meld with "barmaid" which is where I was going—though please do not stop to inquire why. Assuming you've remained awake through the reading thus far.)

Madness. Sheer madness. It's this magical quill, I assure you.

So have you decided Mr. Shakespeare might, after all, suit your stringent literary tastes? How wonderful I am sure. (And I vow that's not a single speck of sarcasm you perceive. Not a single, solitary one. All right, perhaps a half.)

Shall I share a few lines of my own with you? Ones composed during my childhood? Or might you think less of me when you see how very, ahem, <u>less</u> is my talent?

I will refrain from troubling you with them unless you ask.

Thea (who vows she hasn't smiled, or written, this much in an age)

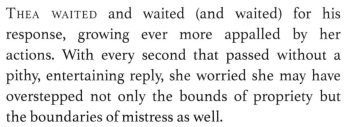

THEA WAITED and waited (and waited) for his response, growing ever more appalled by her actions. With every second that passed without a pithy, entertaining reply, she worried she may have overstepped not only the bounds of propriety but the boundaries of mistress as well.

So it was with complete and utter dismay, and an impressive (and instantaneous) elevation of spirits, that she received not one but *two* notes in response.

Both delivered at the exact same moment.

And both *by* the very man she'd been afeared of offending.

DANIEL WAS GREETED at the door by Samuels, a strapping man of early-senior years possessed of a barely perceptible limp and few hairs atop his balding pate. He'd met the couple briefly upon his leave last night. Recognizing how they'd roused themselves from sleep upon his departure, Daniel had simply thanked them for having the room prepared on such short notice and bid them good night. Now that it wasn't after one in the morning, the latest servant in his employ seemed inclined for a more effusive greeting.

"Come in, my lord, come in," Samuels encouraged without preamble, opening the door wide. "Horrible rains we've been having today, just horrible." It had been raining? He hadn't noticed. "Glad to see it didn't tamper with your plans tonight."

Before Daniel could acknowledge the man—or the weather—Samuels was circling to help remove his greatcoat, talking all the while. "Molly and I have been looking forward to your visit. You'll join Miss Thea for supper this eve?" Samuels came around and reached for gloves and walking stick. With a slight rub of his thumb over the ivory knob, Daniel released it, delighted to find the man so given to jabbering. "Lovely woman, Miss Thea. Hope you don't mind the informality, but she asked us to call her such."

Daniel nodded to indicate his approval. Patting the outside of his pocket, reassuring himself the two folded squares were neatly tucked inside, he inquired, "Where is she?"

He was promptly ushered toward the drawing room. "In here, my lord, in here. Miss Thea?" Samuels called upon reaching the doorway. "Lord Tremayne here to see you." With a polite nod at both, he said, "Refreshments can be served any time you wish. Ring if you have need of us, otherwise we'll be below. Enjoy your evening."

Then the butler was gone, acting as though he didn't know the sole purpose of Daniel's visit was convenient fornication.

The moment she saw him, Thea scrambled from the small writing desk located across the room. Twin spots of fresh color stained her cheeks but he was comforted to see that her smile came naturally and the trembling that had been so very apparent last night was absent.

"My lord." She gave him a deep curtsy, then spoiled the effect by rushing toward him with every appearance of eagerness. Eagerness she checked just three steps away, as though unsure of her reception.

Thinking how easily her inherent splendor over-whelmed the ratty state of her dress—he really needed to buy her a new wardrobe—Daniel covered the distance in one long stride and took hold of her hand. "Thea." He lifted her arm and bowed low before her, straightening and tugging her closer. He'd rehearsed in the carriage so the words came—

almost—easily. "Would ask how you spent your day but think I know."

He couldn't help the grin nor the glance toward her writing desk.

Her feet shuffled in place. He still maintained possession of her hand and she looked at where they were joined instead of his eyes. "Sleeping in, I confess. Then making the acquaintances of the wonderful Mr. and Mrs. Samuels. Exploring my new home." All of that came out in a rush. Only afterward did she meet his gaze, and her breath wafted out on a sigh. "After that I enjoyed the most unexpected afternoon."

Her fingers fidgeted in his and he reluctantly released them, reaching behind his back to clasp his palms together—it was either that or thread his hands through the luxuriant spill of dark hair that was piled up again, but not nearly as intricately as the night before. "Oh?"

"Reading." Her eyes flashed at him. Wondering if he would take up the bawdy banter in person?

With every appearance of boredom, Daniel spun on his foot and walked sedately toward a garish red settee, frowning at the velvet upholstery—at the entire room—once he realized how very vulgar it was, echoing the gold and crimson tones, and the illicit décor, from the entryway.

Upon reaching the settee he planned to banish as soon as he ordered her new furnishings, he sank into a corner, crossed one ankle over the opposite knee, and very casually commented, "Reading? How...droll."

She snickered and he knew she saw right through his act. "Not today. Today I had the most thumping time turning page after page. However"— she started heading toward him, slowly—"just when I was reaching the exceptionally good parts, I'm saddened to say, they disappeared."

"Vanished?" He made a sound of dismay. And decided it was time to share the contents of his pocket. Before he made a cake of himself by talking too much.

"Completely! How shall I ever know *how* the story unfolds if—if—" She stumbled to a halt, both in words and in walking, when he held out the folded squares. "For me?"

Deuced amazing. One would have thought he'd given her diamonds instead of mere dispatches.

"For you," he concurred, making sure she saw what he'd written on the outside of each before relinquishing them into her control.

THEA LOOKED AT THE NOTES, one marked *For Now*; the other labeled *For Tomorrow*.

Two more letters to cherish! How could she be so fortunate?

Not attempting to disguise the smile lifting her cheeks, she tucked the one designated for tomorrow in the pocket of her dress and unfolded the other. Standing just shy of the settee where Lord Tremayne sprawled, she began to read, not realizing until she was partway through the first paragraph, that she was doing so out loud.

"*Dear Thea, It occurs to me I was remiss. Unaccountably callous, in fact, and for that I beg your pardon.*

"*Last eve you so kindly saw to my needs while I—*" Here she paused to glance at him over the sheet. Looking solemn but unembarrassed, his gaze unwavering on her face, he nodded for her to continue. She did, unable to help the lowering of her voice as though they shared a secret. "*While I selfishly ignored your own.*"

Her own needs? The page shook—following the tremor of her arm—and Thea resolutely stiffened her betraying limb and her resolve. Her resolve *not* to give in to any missish vapors. Of a certainty she did have needs! How wonderful of this man to recognize that. To *acknowledge* them. Something her late husband had never, never been considerate enough to do.

Granted, she'd not thought to contemplate her needs so soon, given how she wasn't yet attired to receive Lord Tremayne in the boudoir. But she had reveled in the first sit-down bath with hot water she'd been treated to in ages, thanks to the efficient and indulging Mrs. Samuels. The sweet woman had even washed and pressed her dress. Though really— to greet him wearing the same ugly dress? It was not what Thea had planned. But she was clean, her hair simply but neatly arranged, and Lord Tremayne had looked as pleased as she'd felt when Samuels had shown him in.

Taking solace in that, she firmed her voice and read on, again admiring his fine penmanship (which was easier than fully processing what she was saying). "*May I rectify that now perhaps? I need to, you see, for I did not mean to present myself as such a selfish lover. It was most insensitive of me, to begin our new association that way, and I would like to presume upon you to give me this chance to show myself in a better light.*"

Thea was intrigued. Just what was he planning? Eager now to find out, her voice hurried along as she no longer attempted to read with any great skill. "*While I have a prior engagement this evening and regret I cannot stay long, I don't doubt we have ample time for me to illustrate the merits of my apology in the way—*"

Though there was still a sentence or two remaining, Thea lowered the page. After the titillating exchange they'd carried on this afternoon through Buttons, she'd reached a level of comfort with their relationship that perhaps she shouldn't have. She'd assumed he'd stay for several hours, if not the entire night.

How foolish. Just because she'd remained at home all day, rather than trek to her horrid room across town to retrieve her meager belongings (something she'd put off a fortnight if she could), she had to remember Lord Tremayne was a peer. A man with responsibilities and associations far removed from her narrow place in his life.

Take heart, he's here now. "I'm disappointed to hear you cannot remain but I hope your social activities tonight prove enjoyable. It was very kind of you to stop by given your commitments else—"

"Kind?" he laughed. "Nothing of the sort." A look of mischief entered his eyes. And his posture wasn't quite so sanguine. "Read on or I might lack sufficient...time."

She muttered through the last line until she found her place. "*Illustrate...merits...of my apology in the way of your interpretation of Hamlet and his maiden—*"

The page fluttered from her fingers. "Lord Tremayne!" That was all she said. All she could say, for he surged to his feet and caught the note before it hit the floor.

Holding her gaze, he refolded it, precisely creasing the corners before slipping it into her pocket along with the other. Then he promptly took up her hand, placed it in his, and led her out of the room and directly up the stairs—after no more than a single wink.

He knew he'd shocked her speechless. Good.

Five hours of swapping stimulating raillery had him stiff and ready and craving the taste of her. Had him stopping by now, *before* his dinner engagement, instead of after, when he'd be too tempted to stay the night—and be selfish all over again.

He'd gotten off to a rotten start last eve, Daniel

knew. But he thought their exchanges today had more than made up for it. Beyond his wildest dreams, in fact—her replies had him smiling and laughing and watching out the window for his footman's arrival like a callow youth in the throes of his first passion.

Daniel thought Thea might be beginning to *like* him and damned if he'd do anything to interfere. So if last night was for him, then tonight was for *her*.

Tomorrow night could be for them both.

They reached the landing and he turned toward her bedchamber.

"Nay," she gasped, digging in her feet and pointing down the hall. At his raised eyebrow, she released her bit-upon lips and said in a breathless voice, "The master chamber. I— You— There's a *mirror!*" she finished on a hushed squeak.

A mirror? Grasping her meaning immediately, her hand still tucked snuggly within his, he marched down the corridor until coming to the room he'd briefly glimpsed in shadow the night before. The candles were already lit, several of them, and the bed was turned down.

He released her near the giant canopied bed and leaned in to look up. Sure enough, a large mirror hung overhead, securely fixed beneath the canopy. Five by six feet if it was an inch, and Daniel's body responded as any red-blooded male's should. "D-d-damn."

She'd come up behind him and placed one hand on his shoulder. But her exclamation of "'Tis something, isn't it?" had gotten severed by his curse.

She jerked back in surprise and met his gaze when he straightened. "You don't like it," she said flatly. "You hate it. Forgive me. My room is fine. Let's—"

He gripped her around the waist when she would have fled. Pulled her spine flush against his chest and leaned down to whisper in her ear. "Love it, I...do." He fancied a tremor racked her frame from the breathy caress of his words. Or perhaps it was caused by his hand, the one not across her middle and edging toward her breast, which couldn't help but mold to the firm flesh of her right buttock and thigh. "I'm upset...at not having...time to make long and loud and lusty use of it...tonight."

At his explanation, his kneading fingers, she melted into him. "Tomorrow night, then?" she asked on a lilt, one that had him cursing again—this time his sister and Wylde for tonight's dinner invitation issued last week. Given the strained relations he'd witnessed yesterday—God, had it been just yesterday?—there was no way he could avoid going this evening.

Nothing that would keep him from returning tomorrow.

In answer, he kissed that delicately sweet spot where her neck met her shoulder, ready to swear anew at the high, unyielding neckline of the deuced dress. "Wardrobe," he murmured as his fingers started crawling over and lifting the dense fabric of her skirt higher and higher. "Need to b-banish yours to the grate."

"Aye, likely I do." It was a heartfelt sigh and he was thrilled when his erection rubbed firmly against her back and she did no more than lean in closer to him. "But—but I haven't changed yet into—"

She went rigid. A second later she spun to face him and put her arms in between them as if to ward him off. "Wait! The night rail you sent this morning —I forgot to thank you in all the fun of our earlier exchanges. I wanted to put it on—wear it for you—"

"No time." Gad, if he saw her in that scrap of nothing, he'd never get out of here.

GLOSSING over her forgetfulness as though it mattered naught, Lord Tremayne curved his hands around her waist and boldly tossed her straight on the bed. A coil of naughty desire wound through Thea.

It intensified when he climbed up after her.

She scurried backward until the pillows against the ornate headboard prevented further retreat. Instinct—and modesty—had her clutching her dress near her hips, had her protesting. "You cannot mean to—"

"I can." He pressed inexorably forward, advancing until he grabbed her ankles and spread her feet so he could settle his bulk between her splayed legs. Her skirts rode up as he did so, obscenely so.

Feeling vulnerable, Thea told herself she should protest more stringently, claim she wasn't ready for such perverted intimacies, not without at least *some* preliminaries. She should cry out that she truly did not want this—his powerful torso forcing her legs wide.

But all of that would have been a lie. For she'd already admitted, when she shamelessly wrote those illicit lines this afternoon, that she *did* want this, was vastly curious about the sensations his mouth on her might bring forth. She wanted to experience the scrape of his whiskers in a place that had never known the light of day—much less the lust of a candlelit bedchamber.

So Thea did the only thing she reasonably could —she looked upward.

And what a sight she beheld.

His cigar-brown tailcoat, fitted to perfection across the broad expanse of his shoulders and practically glued to the slope of his tapered back; buff breeches molding to strong thighs... His elegantly attired masculine form—so very dignified for an evening out—so indecently centered between her stocking-covered legs.

Legs that quivered beneath the upward stroke of his hands. "Can and will," he said in a low rumble that sent a fine tremor through her. "For *you.*"

"But I don't—" Thea broke off, seeing her white-knuckled grip on her skirts slacken. Seeing her knees bend, her thighs stretch to welcome his proximity even more. Seeing him pause, tilt his head toward hers.

"Thea?"

She refused to lower her gaze, transfixed by their reflection. Too busy watching his fingers, strong and powerful, slide higher until they gripped the skin of her thighs above the aged stockings. Feeling his hands tighten, then tighten again, until she was persuaded to lower her gaze from the mirror and meet his.

This strong, handsome protector (aye, *handsome*, for the short beard troubled her not a whit tonight) whose penmanship and the personality it portrayed snared her interest when they were apart, but not nearly as much as his presence captivated her completely. Enticed her mind until she thought of naught but pleasing him. Pleasing herself.

Soulful brown eyes narrowed even as he climbed his fingers upward, honing in on that unexplored territory. A quick, fumbled, under-the-covers mating from Mr. Hurwell, with him in his nightshirt and her in her gown, compared naught to *this*.

"You," Lord Tremayne said deliberately, his face looming closer as he closed the gap between his fingers, intensifying the depth of carnal awareness between them, "...don't...?"

Thea's lashes slammed down. Her traitorous, treacherous hands abandoned their hold on her skirts and instead curved over his shoulders, latched on to the solid muscles there. But that wasn't enough to stop their restless wandering and soon they were plucking at his immaculate neckcloth. Tendrils of arousal weaved through her, growing tighter every silent second.

"I don't…" *Want this.*

Liar! You know *you want this. Precisely this. After what you saw at Sarah's party, what the verses made you think of today—after what* you wrote *to him! You* want exactly *this.*

Aye, but I didn't expect it tonight!

One of his large hands left its intimate mooring high upon her thigh and Thea whimpered at the loss. Only to feel those same fingers edging past the opening in her drawers.

Her eyes flew open.

He was still staring at her face. "You say…" One fingertip brushed lightly down her cleft, barely making contact, fluttering through the tight curls and making her feel the caress deep inside. "Say 'no', and I shall stop." Then it brushed upward.

Thea's pelvis tilted forward a fraction, determined to receive the caress again.

When his head flinched, she saw her fingernails had embedded themselves in the skin above the starched silk neckcloth. She relaxed her hands and brushed back a thick lock of coffee-colored hair that had made its way across his cheek.

"Nay, I cannot say 'no'." At his supreme smile, she confessed, "'Tis all so very new to me though."

He slid another finger inside the slit and whispered them both down one side of her sex.

"I know." His breath brushed over her abdomen

as his other hand released her thigh to part the placket shielding her, exposing her completely. Thea gulped as he hitched his entire body closer.

But her legs had no such reservations, widening to make room. As though compelled, she returned her gaze above, to the sight of her stark face, eyes luminous and larger than she'd ever seen them, and his broad-shouldered body, his head only inches from where she craved his touch so very much...

"Let me?" The warmth of his words stroked her damp flesh and Thea jerked a clumsy nod.

THANK THE SAINTS. He couldn't have waited another second. Not with her clean, musky scent luring him onward.

Daniel couldn't believe he was here—with her—on a bed and keeping his clothes resolutely *on*. The linen cuffs of his shirt extended from the tight sleeve of his evening coat, emphasizing how absurd it was —his rough, callus-worn fingers upon her satiny skin. Or mayhap, instead of absurd, he meant *arousing*.

Had he ever arrived at the abode of his mistress with the intent to keep his cock tucked away while dancing attendance on *her* body?

With his thumb, he stroked the smooth, white skin of her upper thigh, nearly choking on his desire when she whimpered and a fresh wash of dew coated the fingertips grazing her furrow. As though determined to thwart him, her thin drawers kept her mound hidden. But the sex-swollen folds were readily apparent, moist and silky and so, so inviting...

He pressed one finger deeper and was rewarded when her nails gouged his neck again.

Her musk grew stronger, his fingers damper, and he slanted his hips until his erection pressed firmly into the mattress, wishing it was her velvet recesses he stroked with his cock.

Alas, his tongue would get the pleasure tonight.

He withdrew his fingers and spread the placket open. Just before he made contact with the honeyed folds he'd revealed, a stirring raised the fine hairs on his nape. Daniel glanced up, only to find her gaze focused not on him—as he'd suspected—and not *closed*—as he'd expected—but instead, her wide-eyed attention was riveted to the canopy overhead. Directly where the giant mirror was secured.

So his new mistress liked to watch?

That knowledge sent flares of desire spiraling through him. Her plain stockings were already in shambles, her drawers freshly washed but old and thin. He planned to buy her new ones anyway. So, without a speck of remorse, he let his primal side have its way.

"Here..." he breathed, leaning back to grip both sides of the slit in either hand. "Shall I..." *Improve the view?*

Rrrrriiiiiip! It was nothing to tear the fragile seam. Nothing to push her dress high toward her waist, nothing to lift one of her thighs over his shoulder and angle his body so she could truly see the show.

But, oh gad, oh God, was it something to hear her shriek turn to a moan when he lunged forward and plastered his lips to her wet heat.

Was it something to finally taste his new lover's flesh, the salty essence of her ardor.

Like a demon possessed, his tongue sought out her flavor, working up one side of her passion-soaked labia and down the other. Availing itself of every drop of silky want she exuded.

Blazing ballocks (his were, of a certainty), she *wanted* him tonight. Wanted what he could give her —his body thrusting into her, creating its place in hers. Wasn't beset tonight by nerves that inhibited her innate response.

Nay, oh nay. She was passion personified, pure responsive female in his arms tonight. And after nothing more than the transfer of a few titillating letters?

He should take pen in hand more often.

Her slippered foot rubbed frantically over his back. Her hands swept over his head, through his hair. Her hips rocked, matching the avid sweep of his tongue as he licked his way to the top of her sultry sex where he delved deeper until locating the tiny pearl secreted within.

While circling the hard nub with the tip of his tongue, Daniel parted her downy folds with several fingers. He discovered her wet and ready, ravenous even—if the encouraging little gasps she made were anything to go by as his mouth silently spoke for him, in all the ways he usually couldn't.

The faster his tongue lashed, the more she tried to clamp her legs together, to escape backward. But his unrelenting hold prevented retreat, kept her in place for his dining pleasure. By God, his mouth might betray him at every turn but not tonight—not in this. When it came to sampling her body, enticing her cream to flow thick and hot, for once, his lips and tongue were in command.

And demanding surrender had never tasted so sweet.

Keeping a firm grip on her thighs, he coaxed the pearl out and placed his lips firmly around the responsive bundle.

"Oh, Lord—" The words were a delightful little whimper, soft and full of air.

He slid two fingers into her damp passage, reveling in how the warm walls drew him in, the muscles of her channel clasping hungrily at him.

"Oh, Lord—" Louder this time.

Daniel started to massage her from the inside, nearly smiling at how she was calling on divine deliverance.

But as he sucked hard on the tiny knot and swiveled his fingers against their own sweet heaven, it was as though his shaft and not his hand plunged through her depths. Amazingly, his primed pipe felt every squeeze and contraction his fingers and lips experienced. Felt her reactions intensify just before she rewarded him by exploding on a scream.

A scream of, "Tremayne!" and he realized she'd been calling on him, praying to him for release. Every sexual atom of his being—the nonsexual ones too—seized in a pleasure so intense, so unexpected, damned if his hips didn't flail, his body bucking against the restrictive garments as he rode the damn mattress until he screamed and creamed too.

Right in his bloody breeches!

Deuced amazing.

But it was her shout of satisfaction that roared through him more than his own release—embarrassingly satisfying as it'd been—because she was still clutching at him, his head, his shoulders—his back with her leg. Her sex still convulsing around his fingers, vibrating against his tongue.

Her mouth murmuring shakily, "L-Lord Tre... Lord... Tremayne. Come...higher. Please."

With one last, lingering kiss to the pink and pouty valley—a kiss of promise to return soon—he answered the frenzied motions of her hands, the sultry plea in her words, and crawled up over her chest, pressing her deep into the pillows.

"Aye?" His own syllable was tellingly breathless. "You rang, milady?"

Her bright eyes found his and she circled her arms around his neck, pulling him down. "Oh, thank you! Thank you," she exclaimed into his ear. "I didn't know—hadn't ever—oh!"

Lower, her abdomen lurched toward his body and she gasped and trembled yet again. Hugged him tighter, with both arms and legs, as her pelvis ground solidly into his groin. "I-I didn't know."

He'd suspected as much but having it confirmed made him hurt—for her.

Daniel tugged one of her strangling arms away from his neck and rose on to his elbow. With his free hand, he smoothed the fallen hair from her sweat-dampened face, ran his thumb over her plump lower lip. Which wasn't so plump, after all, upon such close inspection.

In actuality, her top lip, though alluringly curved, could be described as thin. It was the difference between the two that captivated him, the gentle and unexpected swell of the bottom lip that made him hungry to touch, lick and taste. To explore, plunder and plunge within.

Gad, how he wanted to dive inside her mouth, kiss her with everything he had—his tongue, his heart, most of all his cock.

Hearing her admission touched him deeper than any release—pending or otherwise—and he knew tonight was not the time. "Your husband was a..." *Bastard! A doltish groutnoll.* Not to cherish and charm such a pleasing, passionate creature. Words he would have loved to utter. But he settled for, "A chub."

She gave a tiny shake of her head but didn't try to subdue the blossoming smile. "Nay, he was decent enough. Just uninspired in the bedroom." Her lashes veiled her eyes when she added, "In everything, truth be told."

"A clump," he told her with conviction. Then he dropped his forehead to rest on hers. "Thea." Daniel licked his lips, tasted her all over again. His softening erection surged against her honeyed center, so moist and receptive—thanks to his efforts and her wondrous response. Had a man ever been blessed with such an exquisite mistress?

He forced his hips back and she instinctively followed, wringing a deep groan from his throat, one that originated in the vicinity of his blazing ballocks. "Thea! I must go. I..." *Don't want to.*

Damn, how he didn't want to. But it was for the best—if he stayed, they'd talk more. Either now or later, and he could only hide his defect for so long.

With Louise, it had been easy. She prittled and prattled on about anything and everything, not really caring, and certainly not curious what his views were—on anything—or how he spent his time. With Thea, soft, sexually un-awakened Thea— though he'd certainly awakened her tonight, he couldn't help but acknowledge with a surge of pure male pride that had his cock stiffening within its sticky confines—with her, he had an urge to *discuss*. To ask for details on how she occupied her day. To seek her advice on matters troubling him.

To beg her to massage his shoulders and neck— much as she was doing now—but with his shirt and coat *off*, with him not feeling the pressure of the upcoming evening in the company of two people he cared about and had *thought* happily settled.

"Gad, how I d-d—" *Don't want to leave.* He

masked the slip by kissing her nose, then by whispering his new favorite word. "Thea."

Had he ever loved forming syllables as much?

She leaned forward and pressed her lips to his jaw. "'Tis all right. I know you have commitments outside of our...um...ah..."

"Friendship?" he hazarded, rewarded immeasurably when she nodded beneath him, when she stroked his shoulder down to his biceps as though she wanted more than anything else for him to linger all through the night.

"Aye, friendship," she confirmed without a hint of hesitation. "*Passionate* friendship."

He laughed and kissed her cheek, then hauled off her. As it was, he'd need to return home for new breeches before venturing out again, and if he didn't leave Thea's presence now—all tempting and warm and flushed from release—he'd surely miss dinner at Ellie's...and that wouldn't do.

He already had enough guilt heaped upon him by his wretched conscience, based on how things had gone with Tom Everson the previous night, to invite more regret.

Marshaling his strength, Daniel gained his feet and turned to her. She'd flung her dress down to hide the treat he'd just dined on and her color was as high as ever. But she held his gaze. "Thank you, my lord, for a most, um...erotically enjoyable evening."

"'Twas my...pleasure." He gave her his most formal bow, even clicking his heels together to the accompaniment of her chuckle. Straightening, he vowed, "Until...tomorrow."

"You'll be back tomorrow?" Every blasted minute he had to endure in his release-ruined drawers was erased right then by the solace of her sweet smile. "Wonderful."

"In...deed. I shall count the hours."

"As will I."

2

EXPECTATIONS MOUNT, ONLY TO BE DEALT A CRUSHING BLOW

7:21 A.M.

Though the looming clouds promised another drizzly, grey day, Thea awoke feeling as though rays of sunshine frolicked across her bed, as though a flock of songbirds chorused within her breast.

7:37 A.M.

"Has there ever been a lovelier morning?" she greeted Mrs. Samuels as she descended the stairs.

"The follies of youth must be upon ye, to welcome such a morn with open arms."

Undeterred, she patted the pocket that held the two folded notes Lord Tremayne had given her the night before. "Folly or a blind eye," Thea excused, pausing when she reached the bottom of the staircase and noticed the laden tray the woman held. "I confess, my attention 'tis on a letter I must compose. My, you've been busy, to cook so much this early."

Her new housekeeper's smile contained a wealth of understanding. "I hoped the scents of a hearty meal might lure you awake. And *must* compose?" The woman chuckled. "Like as not you cannot wait to begin. Aye, I know to whom you're writing with such haste. Think ye I missed that rascally Buttons sitting in my kitchen twice over yesterday? Here now, I was bringing up your breakfast—"

"For *me*?" Why, there were no less than five full plates: fried ham, shirred eggs, tarts (strawberry this time, judging by the heavenly scent), kippers, high stacks of bread and more. "I thought all that was for Mr. Samuels and yourself."

"Ye'll please both me and my Sam by making a noble attempt to clear each and every plate." While Thea sputtered, the housekeeper surveyed her with grandmotherly affection. "Child, a brisk wind would keel you over. Breakfast first and then I'll see you settled at your desk with a pot of hot tea."

"You're too kind." When Mrs. Samuels would have headed toward the formal dining room, Thea stopped her. "Nay. I'd prefer to eat in the kitchen. With you both."

"Kind?" Mrs. Samuels clucked, spinning around and heading back down the stairs. "You're easy to care for, I daresay. Our last mistress, God rest her rotten soul, was a crotchety crone. Always ready to harp a complaint but nary anything else. You're twice the woman she was even if she did have the title 'Lady' before her name."

8:24 A.M.

The hearty breakfast consumed (between the three of them once Thea persuaded the couple to join her), Thea slipped into place at her writing desk and readied her quill, letting the anticipation mount. She couldn't wait to read the remaining missive from Lord Tremayne.

She opened the *For Tomorrow* page and, after smoothing the creases with a palm that tingled as it came into such close proximity to his words, began to read.

Thea—

Never fear that <u>anything</u> you care to impart would be unwelcome. As to poetry by your own hand? I am agog with impatience to read what shall no doubt be a sublime and impressive effort. Write on, fair one...

Pertaining to the barmaid comparison you so indelicately suggested—put those pesky one-syllable B's to bed (or perhaps let me escort you there instead?) for you're much too refined to ever be considered thus.

I pray you have fond memories of last evening.

I await with breath bated (and mouth longingly recalling your taste—I hope) for your entertaining reply.

He'd signed it "T", casually, as though they truly were friends.

It was but a moment before Thea's quill was soaring across a fresh page.

For shame! Talk of escorting me to bed, tut-tut. (Though I must be shameful as well for I think of the same—with a frequency I might find alarming had you not mentioned it first.) For double shame: mentioning—and before it even occurred—what your mouth did last night, where it ventured.

Really, Lord Tremayne!

With naught but a parenthetical aside, you whisk me upstairs and beneath the mirror, my limbs quivering so that one would think I am cold. Alas, no. You heat my insides to sweltering with the bold strokes of your pen (and your tongue) but I shall endeavor to cool myself off.

Quickly now.

There. I've raised the window so the invigorating breeze can blow hither and thither my overheated yearnings. Yearnings that only deepen as memories (yes, I confess to many where last evening is concerned) besiege my brain, rendering me—

"Aaaaa-chooo!" As the wind turned frigid, the unexpected sneeze caught her off guard.

Ack! Rain droplets pelt the sill and now the floor and—

8:41 a.m.

When a second sneeze followed the first, she hurriedly closed the window, coming back to her chair and seeing with dismay three ink blotches caused by renegade rain, as well as how much of the page she'd taken up—with lurid flirting!

What would her mother say?

She'd be pleased pink you've found someone to be yourself with and you know it.

"But such a naughty self?" Thea whispered, blotting the worst of the mess from the page. "Who knew?"

There now. I've ceased allowing the rain into the room and onto the page, and now I must cease my chatter. Else how will I ever complete this missive during daylight hours?

You state without equivocation (I feel compelled to remind you) that you would like to be privy to my early compositionary efforts. Please bear in mind, they came to the fore shortly after I celebrated my ninth birthday.

And so, my lord, due solely to your encouragement, I shall mitigate my pending embarrassment and share my poetical talents, minimal though they are:

Drip. Drip. Drip it goes.
All day long, it grows...
The pile, the dripping,
Gluey, sticky pile...from his nose.

A sonnet (or is it an ode?) dedicated to Mr. Freshley of the Dripping Nose.

Thea (who will hurriedly blow hers and hope she's not given you a dislike for her magical quill—or her taste in literature)

8:53 A.M.
     She sat.

8:56 A.M.
     And sat some more.

9:02 A.M.
     Prowled across the room. Looked out into the empty hallway, scowled at the stairs leading down to the footmanless kitchen. Scowled again toward the closed front door. She returned to her drawing room and sat down again.

9:04 A.M.

She waited. Contemplated. Huffed a hearty sigh. Drank a delicious cup of the rapidly cooling tea.

9:11 A.M.

She stood and crossed the room again (twelve times to be precise). Then her posterior greeted the chair once more where she cogitated further on exactly *what* to do with her reply.

For once, there was no one waiting in the wings to deliver it. No exuberant, button-eating youth ready to speed it to its recipient. No stern-faced, kind-hearted man reaching out to receive it in person.

Nay, there was simply one lone (and swiftly growing frustrated) "virgin" mistress wondering what the deuce she should do.

9:18 A.M.

Her foot tapped a jittery tattoo upon the rug. Her fingers drummed upon the sealed note—and with sufficient agitation to rattle the desktop. Her breath heaved forth like an angry horse blowing steam.

9:41 A.M.

"Hummmmmmmmmmmmm."

Drat. Only thirteen seconds.

.   .   .

9:42 A.M.

Deep breath. "Hummmmmmmmmmmmm."

Better. Seventeen this time.

9:43 A.M.

Here we go. "Hummmmmmmmmmmmmmmm-mmm-egck! Eeegkk!!"

Knock. "Why, Miss Thea, you're turning blue! Here now, borrow one of my shawls. And I'll warm ye some more tea."

9:50 A.M.

9:51 A.M.

Did she smell peaches?

9:52 A.M.

9:53 A.M.

9:54 A.M.

Had she ever checked a clock as frequently?

9:55 A.M.

Hated contraptions.

9:56 A.M.

She should have dismantled this one an hour ago.

9:57 A.M.

Well now.

Just what the devil should she do with her note?

9:58 A.M.

Ball it up and have a snack with her tea?

By 10:07 A.M. Thea had swallowed her nerves and snatched up her letter and marched down to the kitchen to inquire whether Mr. Samuels had Lord Tremayne's direction.

"I have an inklin' of his neighborhood but not an exact address," he'd told her. "Before movin' in, we dealt with the agency and his man of affairs, Miss Thea, not his lordship directly. I could inquire, run round to the agency and—"

"Nay. That isn't necessary," she responded, reached for a peach scone hot from the oven, and furtively crept back to her writing desk (perhaps there were unspotted raindrops she could scrub from the rug or the wall).

By 10:26 a.m. Thea had also declined Mr. Samuels' offer of inquiring via his lordship's man of affairs. She'd paced the room another twelve times (times twenty), and watched the clock tick with wretched slowness.

She'd also declined another pot of tea, another scone, and feeling sorry for herself.

Self-pity would never do!

Of course Lord Tremayne would send Buttons by soon. Last eve, he'd seemed as eager as she for their lighthearted correspondence to carry on. She was just being an impatient ninny.

By 10:52 a.m. she was plucking at her dress. Though Mrs. Samuels had laundered it (and even mended the lace Thea had so expeditiously sewn on two days ago), she'd still rather be wearing something else when Lord Tremayne came to call.

He'd surprised her last evening, arriving before she changed into the beautiful night rail he'd sent. What if—

Pure excitement raced through her veins. What if he meant to retrieve her reply personally? What if he were simply waiting until a socially acceptable time to call?

Was she truly expected to wait the entire day before "posting" her note?

Horrors!

AT 11:06 A.M. she jumped up, thinking to dash to her rented room in the unsavory part of London to gather what few personal items she retained. Everything of value had long since been sold, and though a single one of Lord Tremayne's leather gloves (if not a *single* finger on a single glove) was surely worth more than the sum total of all she possessed, the thought of greeting him in something other than her old olive dress drove her onward.

But the reluctance to return there made her pause...

The thought of visiting the dingy room threatened to suck dry all the joy she'd felt today. Yet there was one item she'd grieve were it to disappear, which was more than likely to happen the longer she left the space abandoned: her hairbrush, a gift from her mother when Thea was but twelve and right before her doting parent succumbed to a swift illness. The handle was fancy, the boar bristles soothing.

That was surely worth retrieving.

But what if, during her trek across town, she missed his arrival?

At 11:08 a.m., conflicted, she dropped back down.

11:16 A.M.

"No, thank you, I still have this last cup."

11:17 A.M.

"I'm glad my color is better, and aye, the shawl is quite warm. I appreciate the loan of it." *And aye, I've learned my lesson about timed humming.*

. . .

12:24 P.M.

"Thank you. Lunch would be lovely."

"I saw yer eyes spark at those scones. Making a peach cobbler now, I am. 'Tis my duty to fatten ye up."

12:47 P.M.

"Please don't think it's your bountiful offering; I'm simply not hungry. Such a large breakfast, you know."

Such worry-induced indigestion, you know.

1:03 P.M.

If that clock doesn't start ticking with more alacrity, I'll wring its scrawny neck...

1:20 P.M. (and fourteen s-l-o-w ticks of the second hand)

Oh, doom me to Devonshire! I'm turning into Mr. Hurwell!

That unpalatable thought ringing in her mind, Thea returned the shawl (she didn't want the damp weather messing with the fine yarn) and asked Mrs. Samuels if she could spare a hunk of cheese (which the woman did, her perplexity only growing when Thea explained it was for George and Charlotte).

Moments later, she set off, refusing Mr. Samuels' offer of escort, insisting her errand would best be conducted alone. In truth, she would have been comforted by the company, the thought of confronting Grimy Grimmett nearly enough to make her embrace Clock Watching as a full-time occupation, but she was made of sterner stuff than that.

Asides, knowing—and with a great degree of certainty—that she had Lord Tremayne's arrival to look forward to upon her return only hastened her feet once she left her new residence.

Hastened her down one damp street and then another.

Hastened her a bit faster when the tiny drizzle turned to a full-out downpour...

Until Thea realized, more than a little taken aback, that she was totally and completely lost. Lost and without the fare to pay a hack—had she any notion of her new address. Which she didn't.

Middlesex could've been Mercury for all she recognized through her dripping lashes.

Surely she wasted half the afternoon searching for a familiar landmark, but she might as well have taken the slow coach to Scotland for all the good her wandering did.

EARLY THAT MORNING, Daniel received a letter—just not the one he was anticipating.

Dan—

Jackson's — 10 a.m.

P

And people thought *he* was abrupt?

The summons wasn't entirely unexpected. But the timing was. Disappointing, if not downright disheartening.

So instead of whiling the morning away, fiddling with that pesky gear, the one that hung up every time he tried to get Uranus orbiting properly, while awaiting Thea's next missive, he packed up his pugilistic paraphernalia and hied off to #9 Bond Street. Ready to get his face boxed, if not his ears.

It was nearing noon and Penry had yet to put in an appearance. Or grace Daniel with the ragging he knew was coming.

Slam! Daniel got in a solid jab, then danced back on his toes to the cheers of several men who'd gathered to watch when his latest opponent had issued the challenge over twenty minutes ago. Hell, it was the third person he'd sparred with today and he'd hardly even broken a sweat.

Certainly didn't know the name of the prig he currently shared the ring with, some young blood back in town after his Grand Tour. A cocky upstart who'd insisted they fight gloveless, and without wrapped hands, so Daniel would "feel the wrath of my every knuckle plowing into your flesh, old man."

Old man? Who did this coxcomb think he was dealing with? Methuselah?

Daniel owed it to every male with less than three and a half decades in his cup to take the blustery fribble down a notch. And he'd been doing it in style.

Child's play, really.

Ducking, spinning, landing a nice one-two on the chap's not-so-cocky-anymore chin, slowly but surely wiping that smug expression off his face.

Giving his mind way too much time to ponder his friend's unexpected absence.

Was Penry trying to serve some sort of mangled justice by not showing on time? Doubtless, given his cryptic note, he had an earful to deliver concerning the Everson boy. And even though Daniel was no longer a grateful lad of eight, he respected the man enough to listen to any advice he cared to impart.

After all, hadn't it been Penry, back then known to a young Daniel simply as Will, his older brother's best friend, who was the one person at home—outside of Ellie and their mother—to come to Daniel's defense once David was gone?

"Lookit what we have here," Robert had drawled one afternoon shortly after David's death, sliding from his heaving horse and approaching Daniel, who might've sniffed a time or two but was tearless. "A little c-c-c-c-*cry* b-b-b-b-ba-baby!"

"Stop that, Rob," Will had ordered, jumping to the ground and following a bit slower, leading his horse who wasn't breathing nearly as hard. "Quit mocking him. You know he can't help it."

They'd come upon Daniel while riding over the extensive Tremayne estate, lands that, to a playful boy, had once meant fun and freedom but that now provided only silence and solace. Silence from his father's accusations; solace in the form of memories.

Daniel, still grieving the loss of his best friend and twin, had returned to the scene. Only this time, instead of climbing the tree and laughingly daring David to follow, he'd hunkered down at the base and tried not to cry. Tried with such agonizing effort, he'd bitten his lips so hard, two teeth pierced skin.

"M-m-m-m-mmmm*ocking* him!" Robert had chortled, waving a thin stick in Daniel's face, perilously close to his lips. The very branch he'd been using to whip his horse into a lather moments before. "Stupid t-t-t-t-toad. I still cannot believe I'm saddled with the imbecile for a spare."

Robert used the branch to slap Daniel on the head, prompting the little boy to scramble to his feet. But he held his ground, proud. Not a single tear had fallen. Not before and not now. Turning to his friend, Robert continued, both his attack and his hateful tirade. "Papa's livid *he* wasn't the one to fall—"

"Rob, I said to stop!" Will snatched the weapon and snapped it in half.

By now, the stick had landed twice more on Daniel's cheeks, leaving twin red welts. "Hate you!"

"Very good," Robert said snidely, bowing as though he were at court. "You managed that without stammering like a fool. Care to try again? B-b-b-b-bet you can't do it t-t-t-twice!"

"Come on." Will gave Robert a friendly shove toward their grazing horses. "Quit being such a bastard. We don't want to miss—"

"Leave off. He doesn't mind, hardly even notices. Too stupid to care." Robert whipped around and snaked back to Daniel. Where he kicked one tiny ankle, causing his younger brother to stumble to his knees. "D-d-d-d-don't stay out t-t-t-too late. You might get l-l-l-l-lost."

"Good God, you're an evil one sometimes, Rob."

Daniel couldn't miss the look of sympathy Will shot his way before he convinced Robert if they didn't leave now, they'd miss the big race.

Evidently seeing whether Lord Woltren's new phaeton could stay upright on a particularly sharp curve surpassed the enticement of plaguing a younger brother.

Will mounted his horse—and after one last, lingering and compassionate glance at Daniel—turned toward Robert. "You arse—there are days I detest your mean streak."

Robert just laughed and whipped his horse with the reins.

Seconds later, the older boys rode off.

Leaving Daniel no longer feeling like crying. Just angry.

Angry that David had died while Robert lived.

Mean, snide Robert who made fun of Ellie too. Because she dared to be a *girl*, one who'd started sucking her thumb again after the burial just days ago.

Already back on his feet after facing Robert's taunts, only somewhat mollified by the continued influence Will Penry had on his rotten brother, Daniel turned back to the tree.

This time, though, he didn't climb it. Didn't sink down beside it to mourn.

No, this time he *attacked* it. Slapping and pummeling the bark until the skin on his knuckles and palms scraped off and drops of blood flew along with every flush hit. Scratching with his nails at the living embodiment of the one thing he could blame who couldn't take him to task. Who couldn't talk back—or mock him if he was dumb enough to say a single, stupid word.

And then he was crying. Crying so hard he couldn't breathe, could only pound at the tree while sobbing out his sorrow.

Thunk! The side of his right fist slammed into the bark. *I hate my dumb mouth.*

Thawk! He hit again, just as hard. *So I just won't use it.*

Whack! Bam! The left fist followed suit, pain radiating up his arm when it greeted the tree. *Who needs to talk?*

Pow! Despite the broken finger, both hands clawed and fought the offending monster where once two boys had laughed and played. *Pow-pow!*

Oh God. David's gone.

I miss him so much!

Stinging from the punishing blows, his arms slowly gave out. It took everything in him to raise the right one again and land it against the strong tree. *Bam!*

How I miss him.

BAM!

Daniel feinted left when he should've gone right and leaned directly into the oncoming fist.

"Ompfff!" Everson clouted him harder than expected. And he *had* been expecting it, purpose-fully angling into the hit.

It was only what he deserved. A thorough beating for his sorry-arse actions toward the man's son a couple days ago.

Unknowingly or not, with Penry's continued absence, Everson had stepped in to fill the void.

It was nearing 2 p.m. At least by now, he knew what had happened to his missing friend: rumor was Penry's second eldest had received three offers this week—two this very morning. For a man with multiple daughters, this was accounted a very good thing.

No wonder he hadn't put in an appearance even though Daniel had lingered beyond the appointed time, sparring with several others before inviting Everson to join him, only slightly reluctant when Everson had suggested they wrap their hands.

Laughingly, the man had claimed he didn't want Tremayne to be at a disadvantage, sparring with so many today. He had no inkling how lucky he was about to feel, by stepping into the ring with the guilt-ridden lout who'd disrespected and disillusioned his youngest son.

Smack! He twisted to the side, just in time for that one to glance—heavily—off his ribs.

Daniel had been more than a little surprised Everson treated him with the same respect and friendliness as always. So young Tom had kept his mouth shut, hadn't shared what a bastard Daniel had been. Likewise, Penry hadn't said anything to Everson either. Which meant it was up to Daniel to make amends.

Which he'd do, as soon as he could trust his conscience had suffered sufficiently, by way of his body.

Thunk!

"Ay!" exclaimed Everson, shaking out his gloved fist. "Sorry, Tre...mayne." The man was out of breath. Also likely knocked askew by how many he was landing. No matter what side of the fist one was on, a sharp punch was jarring.

Just thinking about Thea kissing things better almost made it worthwhile.

Thea.

His smile bloomed even as Everson landed an unexpected punch solidly on his cheek.

"Eh, now..." Daniel shook his head, rolled his shoulders. Sweat flew from both. "B-been practicing?"

Everson grinned. "That I have."

Good man. *Let him get in a powerful one.* Daniel knew he deserved it.

So he suffered another. Then another.

Then finally started weaving and ducking, fighting back, if only to a point.

Responding automatically now, his body doing what he'd trained it to for more years than he could count, his thoughts flitted back to dinner last night, to Elizabeth's startling observation during the second course...

"So tell me, brother dear, what's put that smile on your face?"

Wylde cleared his throat. "I'm wondering *who* put the gouges in his neck."

Rather than sputter or blush prettily, as she would have in the past, his sister gave him a frank look, one of curious appraisal. "I believe Wylde has the right of it." Though he still sensed a definite air of reserve about her, she left off frowning at his neck and glanced at her husband as though seeking his advice. All evening, Daniel had sensed a new awareness between them. "What think you? Could it be the same person who did both?"

Wylde grinned like a court jester. "Aye. Most definitely. Tremayne—care to enlighten us as to her identity?"

"I would not." And though it galled him to be the source of amusement for anyone, he could withstand the discomfort given how his predicament seemed to bridge a bond—however tenuous—between Ellie and her husband.

"It matters not who she is," Elizabeth said warmly. "If she makes you this content, I like her already."

Content? Was that the strange emotion besieging him since yesterday? Contentment? Nay, for it didn't come close to conveying the hunger he felt to be in Thea's company again—and he'd just left her —"their"—mirrored bed an hour ago!

"Daniel," Elizabeth's enthusiasm arrested his attention, "shall I apply myself to conjuring you a happy ending with this mystery woman?"

Wylde gestured with his fork and his voice held a bit of a bite. "Before you go spreading herbs and blessings to all and sundry, best conjure up one for yourself, wouldn't you think?"

"Wylde!" A sharp tide of crimson swept up Ellie's neck.

He stared at them both. Wylde appeared indolent, relaxed yet alert, his concentration fixed solely on his wife. Elizabeth was ill at ease. Not mad exactly but definitely irritated about something.

Daniel unglued his back teeth. (Easier to snarl that way.) "*What* the d-d-deuce is"—*going*—"on?"

"What's wrong with us?" Ellie interpreted incorrectly. But the gist was the same.

"Eh." A single-syllable grunt that didn't come close to expressing his worry and concern.

Ellie waved her napkin (probably hoping to cool

her face off). "Nothing a little time won't cure, dear brother."

He didn't believe that for a moment.

Wylde put in wryly, "Nothing a few good tuppings won't fix."

Now *that*, Daniel believed.

But the way Ellie was strangling on her last breath told Daniel he'd best lighten the mood. So he twisted his lips into a semblance of a smile. "Pr-pr-pr —" Deep breath, think it out. Quickly now. *Problem?* Nay, already tripped over that one. *Trouble? Difficulty?* Nay. Nay. *Bad time?* Nay times infinity! Shit.

So he barked, "*Things* not flowing 'tween the sheets, that it?"

"Daniel!" Elizabeth shot a panicked glance behind him.

He looked over his shoulder and saw the footman, eyes deliberately averted.

Damn. "My ap-p-ologies."

As though it didn't matter whether everyone was privy to the situation between him and his wife, Wylde lounged back in his chair. He took up his wineglass, letting it sway from a loose hold, giving the appearance of a man without a care in the world. "If you must know, old chap, the problem isn't what happens *between* the sheets, it's *getting* her there: between them."

With a cry, Ellie jumped to her feet, outrage and embarrassment mingled in her expression before she fled, leaving Wylde to plead his passion for all things political, the servants to clear the table around them (neither gentleman being inclined to move, the wine within easy reach and relocating elsewhere an unnecessary effort).

Leaving Daniel to worry over the affairs of men and women—did the course *ever* run smooth? But mostly leaving him to nod and pretend to be listening to Wylde's natterings while instead, he was thinking of Thea. Imagining the following day when they'd again carry on their budding flirtation, thanks to her bewitched quill and his bemused footman...

BOOM! *Ker-thump!*

Pain exploded behind his cheekbone.

Everson put out a hand to steady him.

Daniel blinked. Damn. That'd been the hardest one yet—what he got for woolgathering.

"I'm think...ing," Everson panted, "that's... enough for...one day."

Daniel slung an arm around the other man's solid shoulders. The gesture was one of friendship; in truth, he was still seeing stars and didn't want to land on his face this close to exiting the ring.

The men made their way to a corner and toweled off. Still standing, Daniel addressed his companion, who'd sunk wearily onto a bench. "Everson?"

Everson looked up from where he unwound the wrapping on his left hand, fingers flexing with each freeing revolution. "Aye?"

Daniel opened his mouth to apologize. To confess how rudely he'd treated—

But no. Wasn't that the coward's way out?

It was the man's son he owed an apology to. "Would like...to call. Is t-t—" He scrubbed the damp towel over his throbbing face to muffle the words. "'Omorrow a'reeable?"

"Call? At my *home*, my lord?" He'd obviously flustered Everson. They'd known each other for years and had never once socialized outside of Jackson's or during a rare sit-down over brandy at their club.

Daniel quit hiding his mouth and tossed the towel to an empty spot on the bench. He nodded once. Tried not to look intimidating. Wasn't sure whether either of them could accomplish that feat— they both sported the beginnings of bruises—and where Everson had landed that last hit, Daniel felt the skin below his right eye pulling tight as it swelled; the rest of him felt like he'd been dragged over rocks.

Despite his surprise, Everson grinned. "Certainly you can, Lord Tremayne. The household comes alive early, so anytime after nine?"

As always, Daniel felt the stiff formality that surrounded him. He wanted to ask the man to dispense with his title, to call him by his first name. Or skip the honorary and use "Tremayne". But habit kept him silent. His name was the absolute worst. Couldn't pronounce it once without mangling the bloody hell out of it. So he settled for, "Eleven?"

"Fine. Fine." Everson shrugged into his shirt, only wincing once before emerging from the neckline. "You're, ah, not planning on having another go at me for that last punisher?"

That brought a smile. "Hardly."

Unwilling to linger now that he'd accomplished the first step of the objective that had been weighing on him, Daniel quickly drew on his street clothes and pulled on his boots. Before parting ways with Everson, he glanced across the bench. Waiting until the man glanced up, he said deliberately, "Have your...boy...Tom there."

"Thomas?" Everson reared back as though struck, his eyebrows soaring. "I didn't know you'd met my youngest..."

But by now, Everson was talking to air.

———◦∘◦———

IT WAS sheer luck that brought Thea into safety and the comfort of Sarah's carriage. Well, luck and Thea's lack of a cloak.

"I still cannot believe I saw you!" Sarah exclaimed, using her warming blanket to blot water from Thea's head.

Moments earlier (as Sarah explained the second she hauled Thea inside), she'd spotted a woman who had taken refuge from the rain, hunched and shivering in the doorway of a closed haberdashery. Recognizing her friend, she'd screeched at her driver to halt and had the carriage door open before the wheels stopped turning. "For once you can thank that dress of yours. Even wet that atrocious color is unmistakable."

"Unmistakably ugly?" The words came out near frozen, but inside, the chill of fear that had gripped Thea the last two hours was rapidly giving way to peace. *It would be all right now.* "Th-thank heavens for friends who love to shop!"

Sarah tried to frown but it came out upside down. "How you can jest when your hands feel like blocks of ice, I'll never know." Sarah transferred her attention to chafing Thea's palms. "Gloves, child! How you could go off without those too is beyond me!"

She hadn't. Thea had (stupidly, she realized after the fact) traded them to a street urchin who swore she knew the way to Hatchards, only to lead Thea a merry chase down several streets—ones without a bookstore in sight—before disappearing.

Thea opened her mouth to apologize, for she truly regretted the loss of the beautiful gloves her friend had given her, but snapped it shut when Sarah started up again.

"Why you won't take the cloak and dresses I've offered..." Now that Thea's fingers were flushed a nice tomato color—and stinging like the devil—Sarah took to bundling her in another blanket. "Offered time and again!"

A few months into their friendship, Sarah had positively insisted Thea take a couple of her dresses once she'd realized how sparse Thea's wardrobe. Thea promptly insisted Sarah take them back.

When one eked out an existence in the dingy slums of London, one did *not* arrive home wearing fine quality silk and fur. Not and live to wear the wares.

"'Tis of no matter. Truly, I'm fine. Thanks to your timely rescue," she said and her teeth hardly clattered at all. "Just so relieved to see you."

"You can thank a carriage mishap two streets over. I was heading home but we had to detour through here—what ever are you doing?"

Thea had emerged from the blanket and pushed open a window to view the soggy sight of decent homes rolling by. Shielding the stray but determined raindrops with one arm, she kept her gaze on the houses while explaining, "Looking for my home. Have you any notion where I live—the townhouse I mean? The one Lord Tremayne secured?"

When no answer was forthcoming, she glanced back at Sarah.

For a moment, her friend gaped like a caught carp. "You mean you don't?"

Wet hair streamed in front of her left eye. Thea blinked and hooked the soggy strands behind her ear. "Not the address, precisely. I've been there since the night of your party. I just left today for the first time but failed to note the street and number. Reckless of me, I know…"

Laughter at her own folly, and because she couldn't help but smile as she recounted the last two days, Thea shared much about her time since leaving with Lord Tremayne (but certainly not everything; some intimate memories—and mirrored reflections—were best kept to oneself).

She also shared the last few bites of George and Charlotte's cheese.

"I cannot believe you meant to waste this quality Stilton on two rodents," Sarah said, a true grin on her features. "Especially after how hard you worked to rid yourself of them."

"Not *them*, specifically, just their offspring and aunts and uncles—"

"Enough!" Sarah held out a hand, choking a bit as the last laugh—and piece of cheese—went down the wrong pipe. "Shall I be practical? It seems as though one of us must and due to your mouse mania, the task turns to me. I could bring you home with me, see you dry and warm in a trice, but based on how you've practically fallen through the window twice—"

"I have not!"

"Searching for a landmark, I think I'd serve you best by helping you find your street. Come, tell me what you remember. When you left the party, which way did you travel?"

And so, after ferreting out a few facts and knowing Lord Tremayne wasn't one to scrimp, Sarah proclaimed, "If I'm not mistaken, that townhouse with the overdone Grecian garden you described belongs to Dunlavy's mistress. It was in Belgrave Square. I'll have Peter drive around that way and you can tell me if anything strikes a chord."

The clouds had parted, letting in a few, nearly

horizontal weak shafts of sunlight and Thea eagerly agreed.

"But I warn you," Sarah cautioned, "it'll be full dark in less than an hour."

Ever pragmatic, she acknowledged the time. "I know full well the futility of keeping you and your coachman out much longer. If we have to, you could write to Lord Penry and he could fetch Lord Tremayne—"

Sarah was laughing again. "Penry fetch Tremayne? Which means you have not his address either?"

"Guilty." A flood of heat washed over Thea. "There's more to this mistress business than I bargained for, I admit. I—"

"Tell me of that," Sarah interrupted with an air of urgency. "You spoke of Buttons and the Samuels and delicious meals, but what of Tremayne? Was he gentle with you? Patient?"

"More than necessary, in truth. Why?" Every moisture-laden particle of air settled heavily on her lungs. At once, the confines of the carriage combined with the sudden suspicion and her soggy self had Thea suffocating under her uncomfortable garments. "Did you have anything to do with that?"

"Me? Perish the thought. Now tell me how he's been treating you. Are the two of you getting on?"

Just like that, as though her fairy godmother had waved a wand, the air shimmered and sparkled with all the excitement Thea couldn't contain. "Positively lovely! Oh, Sarah, he's everything I could have hoped for. Considerate and kind—and how he makes me laugh. He possesses a wicked sense of humor."

"Tremayne?" Sarah sounded intrigued. "I know he can bite off a pithy remark on occasion, but I've never thought of him as a mirthful man."

"With me he is. I believe I make him laugh as well; we're well matched in that regard." She thought of their ribald Shakespearian exchange the day before and didn't attempt to subdue her own smile. "And the home he procured for me? It's the grandest place I've ever lived. All gold brocade and crimson velvet and giant—"

Mirrors. Which Thea swallowed at the last second. "To be sure, I find Lord Tremayne thoughtful and generous and his inexpressibles you mentioned—" She heard herself prattling on but couldn't seem to stop, not even when venturing toward such an inappropriate subject. "Well, I needn't expound upon how happy he makes me in that regard."

Granted, she'd yet to actually experience the full measure of his "inexpressible", but she had no doubt when the time came (which she assumed would be soon—tonight?) that the particular encounter and resulting sensations would rival what he blessed her with the night before.

Instead of being delighted at Thea's good fortune, Sarah only eyed her critically. A look of censure—or was it resignation?—found its way to her friend's expression. "It's only been, what? Two nights? And you're waxing on as if you've fallen—Nay. I won't tread that path. But, Dorothea, mind, don't lose your heart to him."

She waved the concern away. "Of course not! We've only just met."

But was he married? She opened her mouth to ask but Sarah cut her off. "Heed me well, dear. Take joy in your new circumstance and pleasure in his company, but don't mistake your interactions for anything more than what they are: he's *paying* for your services. It's naught but a business transaction, though I admit, a singularly intimate one." Avoiding Thea's gaze, Sarah spread out one gloved hand and began straightening the soft leather where it stretched over every fingertip. "We can delude ourselves and paint it up pretty as a tulip but it doesn't change the facts—women who are paid for sex are, at heart, nothing more than whor—"

"Don't say it! Really, Sarah," Thea remonstrated, more than a little astonished at hearing her friend speak thusly. "*At heart*, I was a woman in need and his money has provided for those needs. 'Tis all."

"Well, make sure you don't lose yours."

"Of course not," she said again, turning once more to gaze out the window. "I know better."

Oh, but hearts to Hertfordshire, she was playing herself for a fool if she truly believed that.

YET AGAIN LORD Tremayne came to her rescue. For not five minutes, and at least fifty unspoken self-recriminations later, she spotted not her new town-house exactly, but the man who'd leased it for her.

"There he is!" she said urgently, so relieved every concern about her heart took wing. "Walking up to the porch— Lord Tremayne!"

While Thea gestured wildly as though she could halt the horses herself, Sarah knocked on the roof, alerting her driver, and leaned forward so she could see. "'Tis him all right. His silhouette is rather splendid."

They neared and Thea's shouts captured his attention. Though the evening light was hazy, and his face shadowed by his tall-crowned hat, when he swung round, she could easily make out the grimace distorting his features. "Oh, dear."

"What is it?"

"He looks angry."

"I'm sure that's simply worry over where you got off to," Sarah consoled, already relaxed back into her seat. "Oh, I've been meaning to tell you, I'm jour-neying to Bucklesham to visit my sister. She just sent word her baby came early and—"

As they rolled closer, Thea saw that worry was the least of it. "Egad! It looks like someone took a mallet to his face!"

"What?!" Sarah flew forward and jerked the curtain aside. "Dammit, Penry!" she swore, startling Thea's head back around. "He *promised* he'd exercise restraint."

"Did Lord Penry do this?" Thea was aghast. She'd never before heard her friend curse and couldn't fathom Sarah knowing about— Actually *condoning*...

But what did it mean? "What reason would Lord Penry have to attack his friend? To hurt him so?"

Explanations could wait for later! The second the carriage rolled to a stop, Thea was fighting to get the door open. "Lord Tremayne!"

3

ODE TO MACHINES

Happy the Man, who in his Pocket keeps,
Whether with green or scarlet Ribband bound,
A well made Cundum.

Generally attributed to John Wilmot, the Earl of
Rochester; from *A Panegyric Upon Cundum*, circa
1720s, a pamphlet extolling the virtues of condoms.

———————◦○◦———————

IT ONLY HURT when he breathed.

So the unexpected gasp his lungs expelled when
Daniel caught sight of Thea flinging herself from the
carriage and racing toward him cut like a sword
slicing across his ribs.

She looked like sunshine, even when the sponta-
neous smile on her face transformed into a flat line,
even when she came close enough he could see that
the depths of her mossy eyes were drowning in

worry—over him. But neither her fading smile nor the growing alarm dimmed how she lit up his entire day. Amazing really, considering her bedraggled state.

Sludge. Her ugly dress, now soaked and muddy —and torn near the hem, he couldn't help but note, when a fair amount of ruined stocking showed—put him in mind of sludge. Sewer bracken.

Yet Thea outshone it still.

"My lord!" she exclaimed, reaching him with breathless abandon. She immediately lifted one ungloved hand to feather fingertips over his cheekbone. "Whatever happened to you?"

Granted, his eye was halfway swelled shut, but nothing was broken—not even cracked, or so Crowley had assured him when Daniel washed up and suffered the man's thorough inspection before departing his bachelor residence to make the jaunt to Thea's. His tiger had already taken his carriage round back.

Daniel had considered sending his regrets and staying home tonight—not dismaying her with his freshly beat-upon visage—but it seemed his mouth had other plans, ordering his team and driver made ready before he was even dry from his bath.

But Thea—

Dear, battle-worn Thea...

Daniel pulled her fingers from his eye and ran his opposite hand down the back of her head. Straggly strands of saturated hair fell over her shoulder, left an increasingly damp spot over one breast.

A breast with one very beaded nipple. "And you?" he intoned, trying—and failing—to keep the concern from his voice. "You look a fright."

"Me?" She blushed, turned to wave Sarah on and just as swiftly took his hand in hers, opened the door and hauled him inside. "Never mind me, my lord. Your face. What—"

"Oh, Miss Thea." At the sound of them entering, Mrs. Samuels came bustling. "Land sakes, child, we thought to have ye back hours ago. About ready to call out the Royal Navy, we were— Oh." Catching sight of Daniel, the woman skidded to a halt. "Lord Tremayne? We weren't expecting ye so early." Her gaze swung to Thea and she forgot all about him. "Look at ye, child! All—"

"I am fine, truly. Would you send up some warm wash water? Start the fire in my room if it hasn't been already?"

The housekeeper hurried off to do her mistress's bidding and Daniel, silently bemused at seeing this calm, capable side of Thea, waited to learn what she might do next. He was stunned when, rather than direct him to wait in the parlor while she changed, she swirled back to him and cautiously touched the cut beneath his eye. "How you must be hurting. Come with me. I'll see that you're taken care of."

He didn't tell her his face was so numb he couldn't feel a thing. Didn't tell her Ellie's witchy cream had taken away the worst of the sting and blessed him with more relief than he deserved.

Didn't tell her that having her fuss over him

nearly made the pain in his ribs and the guilt weighing his heart all worth it.

Nay, for once, Daniel *gladly* kept his mouth shut. Was at peace to meekly follow Thea's guidance, thanks to her hand wrapped gingerly around one set of swollen knuckles, and let her lead him up the stairs.

FINDING LORD TREMAYNE bruised and battered upon her doorstep had chilled Thea more than her icy dress. When they reached her bedchamber and she saw that though the makings of a fire were in place, the hearth was cold, she drew him straight into the windowless dressing room, which tended to be warmer especially when outside temperatures threatened the windowpanes.

Releasing him, she busied herself lighting candles and then turned to shut the door behind them to preserve what heat remained.

"Well now." She swung back, gazed up. And the look in his unswollen eye—the sight of him, so big and so close—elevated her temperature ten degrees. "Well."

He leaned back against one wall, arms crossed negligently in front of his chest. His neckcloth was as carelessly tied as she'd ever seen it, as though tonight he couldn't be bothered with the intricacies of doing it up proper.

Although "proper" was hardly an applicable term when one considered the rest of him: his face had suffered the repeated application of someone's fist, that was for certain, and he'd used her preoccupation with the candles to dispense with other formalities—removing his greatcoat, tailcoat, and waistcoat. The lack left him looking indolent as he lounged against the wall, more compelling in his shirtsleeves than any man had a right to be.

Thea knew she should be wary of him, feeling guarded and distant. Especially given his ravaged state and Sarah's recent warnings of love and whores (nasty business, that; Thea decided to put it promptly from her mind).

How could she be expected to erect walls between them when his very presence made her both secure and aware all at once? Secure of herself and aware of him. When he made her feel more feminine than she ever had, made her want to be closer to him? Had her, in fact, marching forward and pulling one of his hands free to inspect the damage done to his knuckles.

Before she could *tsk* more than twice, he curved his broad hand around hers and tugged, inviting her to meet his gaze. What she could see of it, the flesh surrounding the one eye so puffy a good portion of it was obliterated.

"There is so much gentle strength in you," she said quietly, feeling the power in the blunt-tipped fingers that held hers. "I don't know *how* I know it, but I know I'm safe, even though your demeanor is so fierce and fearsome."

He tried to smile, but with the swelling pulling

his skin it looked more like a sneer. "Would never hurt you."

"I know that, silly man. You chopped my mutton."

"Eh?"

"The night we met, you chopped— Oh, never mind it. Will you tell me how *you* got hurt?"

She waited but he said nothing.

Her hand grew hot within his hold; her entire arm simmering as he feathered gentle caresses over her skin, parts south flaring to life at the heated look he gave her. But he'd yet to explain. "My lord?"

"Mmm?"

"Did Lord Penry do this? Attack you? Pound your face?"

He shook his head once.

"Are you going to tell me what happened?"

He thought a moment. "I walked into a d-d— *Ow!*" He hissed when she squeezed his fingers at the lie. He finished wanly, "A...door?"

So he didn't intend to tell her? All right, neither did she relish confessing how her blunder-headed afternoon had gone. "A door? One with a nasty streak it appears."

"And you?" he inquired silkily, taking up her other hand and spreading both her arms wide so he could survey her from fallen hair to mud-splattered hem. "Where— What of your...day? Stroll into the ocean? Embrace a shark or...two?"

"Oh, that..." She whirled from his loose hold, too

embarrassed to confess her folly while standing beneath his inspection.

"Aye, that." Lord Tremayne came up behind her, halting her retreat by pulling her spine flush against his chest.

"My lord. Stop. I'm drenched." But she couldn't stop herself from sinking against his strong, stalwart body and her protest was halfhearted at best. "I'll ruin your clothes—"

"Hang my clothes," he said hotly, his breath tickling her ear. He pulled her tight to him with one arm snug across her middle. "Thea—were you set upon by footpads?"

"Nay," she rushed to assure him. "Nothing so dire."

"Attacked by angry geese?"

That had her laughing and hugging his arm. "If you must know, you wretched man, I became lost. Lost in the rain the first time I ventured out and it was—it was—" She swallowed the growing lump of fear, determined not to give in to unrealized *what-ifs*. "'Twas..."

So very frightening. Wandering the streets for what amounted to hours, wondering if I'd ever find my way back. Back home, back to your arms—

"Alas!" She shoved his comforting touch away and broke free, scrubbing at her eyes. "'Twas no fun at all. I detest feeling so very helpless and alone." Hearing what she'd divulged, Thea rushed to cover the admission. Edging farther away, she shrugged.

"Though I hadn't realized it, I must have wickedly awful compass sense and—and—"

The heavy gait of his steps shadowing her gave but a second's warning before he spun her to him again, this time chest to chest.

He flinched and his breath hissed out. But he only held her more securely as his fingers went to the buttons at her nape. "So you d-*did* have a fright."

He swore, but his fingers remained gentle. She stared at the column of his throat, again catching that elusive scent of his and drawing it deep into her lungs. A faint memory teased—

Once several buttons were undone, he curved his hand around the base of her neck. "You're freezing." It was a growl. "Where's that water—"

As though summoned, Mrs. Samuels knocked and forged inside at his brisk "Enter."

She started to step back but he kept her in his embrace.

Both Mrs. and Mr. Samuels came into the small room, carrying steaming pots, which they placed on the washstand. "We'll be but a moment and I'll have refreshments brought to your chamber as well," she told them, kindly keeping her eyes averted. "Sam already has the fire going and the room is warming nicely. Will there be anything else, Miss Thea? Lord Tremayne?"

She let him answer in the negative as her mind was working feverishly, thanks to the spicy scent of cloves and something else, something faint but sweet, taking her back to when she'd first seen him

—when he'd arrived late to Sarah's and had drawn such a chorus of greetings just before sitting next to her.

"Wait." Recklessly, her mind on two different paths at once, Thea called to Mrs. Samuels. The woman popped her head back in and Thea said, "The master chamber down the hall. Please heat it as well."

"Certainly, miss."

Once they were alone, Lord Tremayne went right back to undoing her buttons and she returned to resolving what kept niggling her brain. Astonishingly, the experience of being undressed by him paled as she pieced a large part of the Tremayne puzzle together.

"There now. Lean..." He coaxed her away and started tugging the sodden, tight-fitting sleeves of her dress down her arms. "Forgive me."

His words arrested her from the fact that the bodice of her dress had just drooped forward, leaving her upper half covered by only a damp chemise. That and long, stubborn sleeves, adhering like glue to her elbows. "Forgive you? What ever do you mean?"

"I've..." Though it appeared all his energies were focused on peeling down her left sleeve, Thea had the sense he didn't see his efforts at all, that his attention was aimed inward. "Remiss. Horri...bly so. Not to have stationed a footman here or...assigned you a coachman or—"

"Stop." She was practically giddy. He felt guilty

over not giving her *more* servants? "Remiss? When you've blessed me with so very much? 'Tis I who needs to learn directions. You fight for sport, do you not?"

"There." The left sleeve finally free, he pierced her with his one good—and one swollen-narrowed —eye. "What?"

"You. The bruises." She was so relieved to have figured it out. "Like cockfighting—you fight for sport."

She'd heard of men who wagered on roosters or dogs trained to fight to the death. Knew how popular boxing had become, men actually enjoying hitting each other. She'd just never seen anyone who'd done it, timepieces and Mr. Hurwell's droning diatribes about equestrian races being the extent of her "social" interaction the last few years. "Pugilism," she said with satisfaction. "I'm correct, am I not?"

A slow, crooked grin spread across his mouth as he nodded. "Aye. Like cockfighting," he confirmed, "only with fists."

"As opposed to your cocks?"

Thea couldn't believe she'd said that.

She knew the word, of course. Living in the slums had enlivened her vocabulary if not her life, but she'd never before uttered it.

Lord Tremayne didn't seem able to believe it either.

He stared at her a moment, eyebrows raised, breath held. Then they both laughed. He winced, then laughed again. Thea howled so hard her stomach hurt.

How grand her life had become since meeting him.

In the bedchamber, Mr. and Mrs. Samuels shared a surprised look.

She silently deposited the tray with wine, fruit and cheese and several wedges of roast beef upon the dainty circular table while he—not so silently— set down the bucket of coal beside the hearth and beefed up the flames.

Together they turned and exited the room, securing the door behind them.

It wasn't until they were approaching the bottom of the second set of stairs that Mrs. Samuels spoke. "Didn't his man of affairs lead you to believe that Lord Tremayne was rather a somber fellow?"

"That he did."

"He doesn't sound somber to me."

"Someone needs to teach that boy how to duck."

Funny how breathing without her hurt but laughing *with* her only tickled his ribs. She'd surprised him, this mistress of his.

Had from almost the moment they met.

But something surprised him more when he

freed her right arm—and was confronted with the bruises lining her wrist.

For a split second, Daniel thought he'd been too rough on her that first night. But then sanity prevailed. Lord knew he'd seen enough bruises in his life to know these weren't fresh. Had to be several days old. There were individual finger marks as well as some deeper yellowing, indicating it hadn't been the first time someone had used force on her.

Rage stormed his gut; he hated seeing anyone abused by bullies. He'd lived with it enough as a child, seen how cowed Ellie had been around their father, experienced his own fortitude and will draining away too many times to count to stomach it happening again—to anyone he cared about.

The overpowering need to protect Thea flooded through him.

Her eyes were still sparkling with their shared laughter while he had to exercise every bit of restraint he could summon. Keeping his grip on her loose, he raised her arm between them. "Who... did...this?"

She looked completely startled for an instant, then her eyes flicked to the discoloration before jumping back to his. The laughter withered and she pressed her lips into a tight line.

"Thea?" His thumb smoothed over the old injury, his gaze pinning hers, demanding answers.

He watched her gather determination around her like a cloak. "Nothing you need concern yourself with."

He refused to let her get away with that. Unintentionally, his hold constricted until the subtle start she couldn't hide reminded him to temper his anger at her unknown assailant. "I *am* concerned."

"Just my troublesome old landlord." She tossed her head as though to prove how unaffected she was. The gesture was ruined by a long hank of damp hair slinging onto her shoulder, bringing to mind the day she'd had. "He won't bother me further."

Daniel purposefully gentled his grip, giving no indication how ferociously he wanted to throttle the absent man. "You're sure?"

"Positive."

Despite her tone, he could see the thought of the bastard flustered and frightened her. Daniel would make damn certain no one would ever put that look in her eye again. He'd send Swift John to her first thing tomorrow, tell the boy to stay. From now on, if she needed him, he'd know in a hurry.

Before he could reiterate she was to use the servant as her own, Thea leaned down to step from the sludgy dress. Then she stood, not quite shivering, in her chemise. Instead of meeting his gaze, she addressed a point some three inches above his shoulder. "If you'll wait in the bedchamber, my lord, I'll wash and be out to join you directly."

So that's how she intended to play this? He glimpses a teeny bit of honest fear and she pokers up stiff and pushes him away?

Not hardly. Blocking the door with his body, Daniel jerked at his neckcloth, wincing when his knuckles protested the stubborn knot. Working it loose, he leaned to the side and snared her gaze. "We'll wash together."

He watched comprehension sink in as he dispensed with the neckcloth and undid his shirt cuffs, the mild protest of his ribs worth it when he ripped the shirt overhead and tossed it behind her. Worth it because the prim, detached look dropped from her face and she exclaimed over the fresh mottling on his side.

He'd never thanked a flush hit more.

Stripped to the waist, he reached for her chemise —ready to bare the rest of her—but she hauled out of reach. "Wait. Do you care to tell me *why* Sarah thought Lord Penry did this to you?"

So he is out to smack some sense into me?

Daniel smiled grimly and sidestepped her question. "Never saw him."

"My lord..." There was a threat in her tone, as though she chastised a sword-wielding grasshopper bent on terrorizing her begonias.

The image had him laughing again. "'T-tis true. Crossed paths not at all with him—"

"Nor with a door, I'd imagine."

He had the grace to look ashamed. Why hadn't he just *told* her he sparred?

Because Elizabeth always made it out to be so much more? *Father beat it into you until you came to believe it—you think you deserve being punished because you lived while David died.*

That wasn't true. Not anymore.

However, an uncomfortable piece of honesty made him recall how he *had* thought he deserved a pummeling today for his treatment of Tom.

The sudden burst of clarity was startling.

But it paled when she stepped forward and touched an old scar on his shoulder. "There now. I shall badger you no more. Only tell me what—or who—caused this..."

It was a ragged, several-inch line that Louise had never once noticed or remarked on. Not in all their years together.

"Trouble with a tree branch." When Thea rose up on her toes to rain kisses over the puckered and drawn skin, the rest escaped without forethought. "The day my brother died."

How easily the confession slipped out—physically and emotionally. Part of Daniel wanted to question why it was that touching Thea seemed to loosen his mouth, to make the words come easier. The rest of him simply marveled at the flash of compassion in her expression when she leaned back to stare into his eyes.

"Climbing," he explained. "We were eight."

"Both of you?" She grasped the significance immediately. "He was your twin? Oh, Lord Tremayne..."

The soft sympathy was nearly his undoing.

Daniel, dammit! He wanted her to use his name.

But then her gaze and the light graze of her fingers moved to his lips.

"What about this? How did you scar your mouth?"

Instead of tightening as they always did when he thought of that day, Daniel found his lips opening, confiding, "My father."

"He did this? On purpose?"

He jerked a hard nod and his hands flexed on her waist. How long had he been holding her?

Rather than drop to her feet or back away, she came closer, blessing him with her tranquil presence. Like a man addicted to drink, he craved more.

"I can tell the memory pains you." Her voice became a whisper. "Shall I kiss it away?"

Too stunned to speak, he nodded.

This beautiful, bedraggled woman then began searching out every mark and blemish his exposed body possessed, kissing each, murmuring words of comfort and solace...incredibly, not shying away from his "fierce and fearsome" self.

He was tempted to tell her the truth. All of it. His dreadful difficulties with speech. His—

Don't be stupid! You've known her less than a week.

But still, he was tempted...

Do you want her to think you a fool before you've had time to convince her otherwise?

And still her kisses and caresses continued, up his chest, across his shoulders, down his arms...

It felt as though she were courting him. Courting his mind as she wove a spell over his body. Her unabashed acceptance made him want to give her something in return. He wanted to buy her jewelry and furs, maybe a dainty horse and—

His mind backtracked. Jewelry and furs. "A coat," he interrupted her journey over his raw knuckles to ask. "Have you one?"

"Nay. And my gloves slipped away today I'm afraid."

"Slipped away?"

"On the heels—or should I say fingers?—of an unhelpful beggar..." Once again, she tried to laugh off her troubling excursion.

They hadn't known each other long, but Daniel didn't think Thea was a female given to vapors. She'd obviously had a trying day, and after what she'd just done for him, replaced past hurts with present approval, putting aside his selfish wants was the least he could do.

His entire body tingling from her exploration, he grasped both her hands and brought her fingertips to his mouth. It was his turn to cherish her.

He'd help her bathe. Then he'd take his leave. Let her sleep.

She deserved no less.

"Let me wash your hair." He led her to the basin where the no-longer-steamy (but suitably warm, a quick dip of his finger told him) water waited. There was an empty pail for rinsing as well.

Thinking through his words, he guided her to kneel. "You've had a harrowing...day. I shall..." *Tuck you in bed and bid you* adieu *with a kiss. Dream of you all night long.* "Finish here and leave you...to rest."

Giving in to the pressure of his hands, she ducked her head over the basin so he could dampen the mass.

"By all accounts"—the words were muffled by her position—"I should be exhausted but I'm not." When the warm water streamed over her scalp, she made a low murmur that had his body tightening. "Likely it'll all catch up with me tomorrow. For now I'm quite awake."

THEA BARELY HID HER ASTONISHMENT. He was washing her hair!

A man, a *marquis*, was patiently working soap over her scalp and rinsing the suds away. He was brushing through tangled strands with his strong fingers and massaging her head long after the water ran clear.

Who knew one's scalp was so susceptible to stimulation? Brushing her own hair was a calming experience; having her mother brush it when she was a child, a very pleasurable one. But this?

This was beyond fantastical.

With every touch, shards of lightning struck from the tips of his fingers and blazed a path straight to her stomach, and lower.

From the moment she'd seen him standing on her doorstep, she'd felt invigorated. Now she just felt aroused.

Thea yearned to swing her head back as he blotted the length with a towel, yearned to grasp his muscled arms, pull his chest to hers and assuage the heavy ache in her breasts. The ache his thorough hair washing had created.

And he planned to *leave her to rest*?

Not when the soothing stroke of his hands had energized and enlivened every particle of her body. Not when she wanted him to kiss her and not stop.

Not when she wanted *him*.

"There now," he said as though the task was finished, giving one last squeeze to her hair. And giving her the sense he was about to make good on his promise and depart.

Removing the towel from his grip, she faced him squarely.

After inspecting his body earlier, trying to look dispassionately at each of the imperfections carved into his skin and instead only seeing the man beneath the hurts, she hardly registered the swollen eye or bruised side anymore. What she saw before her was a spectacular specimen of masculinity.

What she wanted was every square inch pressed against her.

Seeing his look of steely determination tempered with a frown of self-denial recalled to mind Sarah's curious words in the carriage. All Thea could think was how he'd not yet truly bedded her. Not completely.

And he was set to deny them both? *Again?* Not if she had anything to say about it.

She'd had enough of being quiet. Enough of not stating her wishes, of blending into the background, first with her husband and then without him. Enough of not being clear about what *she* wanted.

Time to change that, starting now. "Just so we have clarity between us, Lord Tremayne, I am quite willing—more than willing actually—to have you... have you..."

Why was she dithering? *Just say it, Dorothea Jane.* "I would prefer you stay. Would like for us to come together fully." He looked a bit nonplussed. While her fingers strangled the damp towel, she forged ahead. "To be perfectly blunt, I don't want you to leave—and leave me aching again. And after being confronted with your magnificent chest, I'd like to see the rest of you naked, to feel you pressed ag-*ahummm*—"

Without having to finish her pathetic recital, he *knew*. Knew and took command.

His arm went around her back and molded her to him. His mouth sang a symphony of lust against hers.

This kiss was nothing like the exploring ones in the carriage, nothing at all like the sensual one he gave her after bringing her to orgasm last night.

Nay, this kiss was hard and hot, urgent, and just a touch shy of savage.

This kiss boiled her blood and dampened her loins faster than she could think *he has on too many clothes*. As he plundered her mouth with primal intent, her nails scored over the fabric covering his posterior.

With a smothered chuckle at her eagerness, he

gave her lips one last bit of intense suction before releasing them. "Shall I?"

While she struggled to comprehend (and kept clawing at his frustrating pantaloons), he dragged his hands past her bottom to grip the hem of her chemise and hauled it over her head.

"Ah, Thea." He gasped at the sight of her, one unsteady hand going to the ribs discernible beneath her slight breasts. "You're so thin. So dangerously thin..."

She didn't take offense, didn't panic that he found her lack of womanly flesh distasteful. How could she? When the look in his eyes said the concern was *for* her.

He swiftly used the washcloth to cleanse every inch of skin with the remaining water, and then he scooped her up, carrying her through her feminine bedroom and into the hallway where he unerringly made his way to the master chamber.

She spared scarcely a second to wonder at his murmured, "Like Cyclops...just in t-time..." because upon reaching the trysting room, he placed her on her feet and kissed her again passionately. From her lips, to her shoulder, working his way down until his tingle-giving mouth reached her wrist and then to the tips of her fingers. After sucking not one but two into his mouth and rousing an even deeper hunger, he released her, straightening and raking his gaze over her naked form.

She trembled from the heat in his eyes. Trembled more when he bent to bestow a tender kiss on the bruises above her wrist. "So lovely."

A blush threatened but there was no time for modesty. "You still have on too many clothes."

She reached for him but he reached her first, fusing their lips as he used his grasp on her waist to place her square across the mattress. Thea stretched her arms to receive him but he was already skimming his lips down her body as he unfastened his pantaloons, then wrestled with his boots.

His lips stayed busy on the skin of her stomach, tongue circling her navel. She heard the sweet thump of one boot hit the floor. "Hurry," she ordered, that achy sensation growing between her legs. "Just shove them off and—"

He licked lower and her hips lifted off the bed, her nails scoring the counterpane at her hips, wishing they were sinking into his skin.

And then it *was* his skin when he finally shed the rest of his clothes and came down over her, the smooth, smooth skin of his shoulders greeting her fingertips.

She welcomed the weight of his body pushing her into the bed, welcomed the reverent slide of his hand up her stomach until he was moving his fingers over the sensitive peak of one tightly bunched nipple.

"My charms are rather...minimal at the moment." Why did she go and mention that? Even when eating regularly, her "charms" weren't much above *minimal*—but did she have to draw his attention to the lack?

Embarrassed, avoiding what she might see in his gaze, Thea flicked hers overhead. Then promptly forgot to worry about her bosom deficit. Because she was staring at the shadowed reflection of his naked buttocks!

So very pale, so very muscular. So *very* sinful of her, to be salivating over the salacious sight.

Heavens to Hampshire, thank the blazes for the glowing hearth and what it revealed. Her first look at a nude man most definitely did not disappoint. In truth, the titillating sight tripled her ardor in an instant.

Lord Tremayne drew her focus from the mirror when he climbed up her body, wicking his tongue along the path of his fingers until he licked up one barely mounded slope, sending all manner of delight from his tongue to the far reaches of her body. He applied his tongue to the puckered areola and murmured, "Not the size that matters..."

Looking pointedly from her breast to her eyes, he curved his mouth in a slow grin. "It's the cherry on t-top."

Holding her gaze, he closed his lips around one aching nipple and delivered sufficient suction to have her back arching off the bed, her hips toward his, and her neck up so she could watch. Where she blinked in surprise, seeing the length of her body bracketed by his.

Miraculously, she looked every bit as voluptuous

and alluring as her paired portraits downstairs, only instead of burled wood, she was framed by Lord Tremayne's hands and body.

For once, *she* was a naughty nude, and how it made her smile. Made her eager for more, impatient for the length of his erection now pressing into her thigh.

Breathless whispers of encouragement escaped when his lips sucked fiercely on her breast and his tongue flailed over the tip, the flat of one palm coming up to massage the other. "Aye, like that."

Whimpering at how easily his attentions fired her blood, she grazed her hands over his shoulders, coasted them over the powerful muscles and passion-warmed skin, craving him closer...ever closer.

He transferred his mouth to her other breast while his splayed palm glided down her stomach and below her waist. She tilted toward him and was rewarded with the first probe of his fingers.

"Mmm." She dug her nails into his back and crawled them lower as though she could bring him higher, entice his shaft to slide inside.

But wait—

As he stroked over her labia, her thighs widening in welcome, her fingertips encountered more than one straight ridge low across his back. Despite the growing pressure, the languid urgency building in her abdomen, she deliberately traced along one wicked line until encountering a host more, numerous thin welts parading across his flank the farther she slid her palms.

Understanding made her gasp.

Noticing where her hands had frozen, he grew rigid.

"Your father?" she whispered.

A full three seconds later he nodded against her breast.

"That insensitive bastard." Curving her fingers over the scarred flesh, Thea swore aloud for the first time in her life. "How could he—"

Lord Tremayne lunged upward and silenced her with his lips, with the raggedly voiced, "You wonderful woman."

YOU GODDAMN WONDERFUL WOMAN!

The taste of Thea, the feel of her slick passion coating his fingers, her untutored body's response— and her reaction to the old scars—practically stealing his wits, Daniel recalled himself without a moment to spare.

"Stay." The order was instinctive. Rude even, as one hand drifted over her trembling thighs when he reluctantly slid from the bed to retrieve one of the machines purchased the day of Sarah's party.

Another second and he would have forgotten to armor himself.

Startling because after years of regular and consistent use, he never forgot. Never.

He'd started donning the machinery years ago

after it made the rounds when Lord Tims' trusted mistress gave him not only an hour's pleasure but a screaming case of clap (after dallying with a visiting French count, or so the story went).

Not one to risk his ballocks for a quick tup, especially after hearing about the pain and blisters, it had been a worthwhile sacrifice to avail himself of the plentiful preventatives. More than that, it became easy to justify their usage when long-time Louise started hinting at something more permanent between them, offering to bear his heir. Egad. The lunatic ideas she had espoused made it easy to suffer a bit of sensation loss for the sake of his sanity.

So it was with no little astonishment Daniel found himself nearly forgetting a habit so well ingrained. Habit or no, his blighted hands fairly shook at the task, his need for her so great.

At his continued absence, she sat up with a whimper, not understanding his departure. Until seeing what he was about, pulling the device over his cock and tying it firmly at the base.

"Oooo—is that a preventative?" She leaned forward as though to inspect the contraption covering his shaft. "I've heard them hawked in the streets but not seen one up—"

With a growl, he shoved her back and grasped her ankles, one in each hand. "Later."

He tried to apologize and explain a world of information in those two syllables. *Later*, she could inspect the armor if she was of a mind. *Later*, he'd make it up to her for being abrupt. *Later—later—later*, maybe his patience would return.

For now, a savage beast controlled him. A sexual beast she'd roused. One that needed appeased.

"Later," he said it again, softer this time, but it didn't seem to matter. She wasn't pouting—prettily or otherwise.

Nay, she was writhing on the bed, her hands stroking up his arms, nails scraping over his skin, legs tensing within his restraining hold, as he slid his grip along her calves, unable to miss her feminine folds weeping, begging for satisfaction. His recently neglected body was past ready to please her.

Yet he knew if she laid a hand on him again, if she dared caressed his ridged buttocks once more with her delicate touch, it would be over before it began. So he braced his legs wider on the floor and readjusted his hold until he could pull her forward. Positioning her groin right where he wanted it—and his arse out of reach.

Instead of fighting him as he thought she might, Thea only stretched back upon the mattress and urged him on. "Aye, please."

One of her hands fluttered above her stomach. A second later those very fingers came down to knead her breast. Her other hand flew to her mons, then jerked backward two inches, anchoring itself just above her downy curls.

"T-touch yourself for me." He was shaking, his entire body vibrating as she did as bade, her eyelids at half-mast as her fingers edged past the dampened midnight thatch and disappeared into the honeyed well between her legs.

"Ohhhh," she breathed, sounding excited and pleased and more than a little surprised. "I'm *ready* for you."

Meaning she hadn't been with her husband? Or had never been given leave to touch herself to know?

Either thought had pride—and fury—storming through him. That such a responsive, passionate woman would go unappreciated...

"Thea." The cry turned ragged when he saw her fingers emerge from her depths, slick and glistening, only to disappear back inside.

Timing his advance with the steady pace she set, he released one leg to grasp his cock and run the tip over her cleft. For once he hated the cover shielding him from feeling all sensation. So he nudged his thumb forward, let her heat and viscous fluid coat his skin, and imagined that those silky juices of hers flowed over all of him.

Gripping his staff just below the crown, he pressed forward, stroking between her spread labia.

"Yes, please." If one discounted the breathy way she said it, she sounded so very polite and proper, he almost laughed.

But when the leg he wasn't holding curved behind his thighs to bring him intimately closer, deeper—

Thoughts scattered.

Overridden by the sight of her hands delving between her thighs, stroking up his shaft, coaxing him to enter. Eclipsed by the urgency her touch conveyed.

Her lilting cries gave him the strength to advance slowly and then she was killing him, the walls of her sheath opening with such exquisite reluctance as he forged deep, then deeper still, her passage closing in around him and clasping so tight, damned if he didn't spend before ever lodging the full way inside. Before ever pumping out a single stroke.

Damned if skill and experience didn't flee as his cock tunneled inside her rippling sheath with a series of short, clumsy paroxysms that left him gasping for breath—and his balance.

The orgasm tore through him unlike any other.

Tensing his ballocks and his neck as Thea's bawdy bits tightened like a vise, squeezing his cock, his heart, and every other part a man *thought* were his.

Leaving Daniel gasping and shaking—and wanting to tup her all over again.

4

OH, TO BE AN ASS

And will as tenderly be led by the nose
As asses are.

William Shakespeare, *Othello*

———————◦————————

"OH MY," she said when Daniel eased, regretfully, reluctantly, out of the snug haven of her body in stunned, stupefied silence. "Is that all?"

How could he have blasted off so precipitously?

Daniel looked at his recalcitrant cock. Still stiff. Still erect though totally spent. Still primed for more though unmistakable proof of its unruly tendencies filled the reservoir.

Damn me.

Not since first partaking of the sins of the flesh had he stayed so achingly solid after such a powerful ejaculation.

Damn me, he thought again, unsure how to react. The muscles of his legs quivered until he locked them in place. Ground his heels to the floor. He'd be damned in truth before he lost his footing, fainted to the floor like a fribble.

"All right then." At his lack of response (he was still staring at his flabbergasting phallus—until her disappointed sigh pulled his head up), Thea hugged a pillow to her breasts. She was visibly shaking—and not at all satisfied he knew. Thanks to his impudent penis.

"Well," she said with false brightness, "that was, um...intense."

Intense? *That* was how she described their first time together? Not exceptional or pleasing or exceptionally pleasing or—

He must've scowled.

For she immediately added, "*Memorably* intense. Which is a good thing, I vow." Her gaze drifted to his chest and a hint of color flooded her cheeks. "Wonderfully intense, to be perfectly clear. Much, much better than uninspired or uninteresting or...lethargic."

Lethargic? That lummox she'd been married to, no doubt. The man obviously didn't know how to appreciate a woman, even had she been glued to his prick.

Anything but lethargic herself, while holding tight to the pillow with one arm, Thea scrambled for the sheet with the other, giving every indication of jumping from the bed and retreating to her personal chamber.

Time to make something clear.

"Thea?" His voice was gravel but it had the desired effect. Her motions halted. She sank back onto the mattress, still choking that pillow.

She blinked up at him. "Aye?"

"Think you we're finished for the night?"

"We're not?" A hint of confusion came into her eyes before she caught on and a quick smile curved her lips. "We're not. Oh, good."

Aye. He intended for it to be *very* good.

As though she read his thoughts, her mossy gaze fairly sparkled. She released her hold on the pillow. Angling her elbows behind her, she propped herself up and asked brightly, "May I inquire what's next?"

Chuckling over her undisguised relief, he tore off the soiled machine and retrieved another. No time to wash the blasted device now. Not when his lady lust lay waiting.

What was next? she asked. Let him number the things...

FASCINATED BY THE INTIMATE SIGHT, Thea watched Lord Tremayne exchange the used preventative for another. It looked innocuous enough, simply a thin, flesh-colored membrane topped with trailing ribbons. What she knew of the popular machines was garnered from the street hawkers who extolled their various virtues. ("Won't chafe ye partner nor make ye pecker burn!" or "Jumbo superfines, right 'ere, milords! Best armor yer coinage can buy!" and "The finest machinery in London! Double scraped and rinsed thrice! Sold by the fives.") But hearing about them paled upon seeing one up close.

Seeing Lord Tremayne's personal parts up close.

Seeing him cloak his erect shaft with the device, and so soon after she'd touched the sides of it, after having it in her—if for so short a time—brought all the passion and pressure and persistent ache plaguing her loins storming to the surface.

He muttered something like, "Damn me...not supposed to lose my mettle like that," while wrestling with the scarlet ribbon weaved around the opening. His self-directed flagellation made her smile, but she was too enraptured watching the sway of his ballocks, the crisp hair of his groin, the thick erection he handled with such ease, to respond.

Shoving the pillow to the side, she scooted around to recline on the bed properly, with her head near the headboard, where she waited for him to join her.

The room was warm and her body on fire, so she was surprised to see gooseflesh pimpling her skin. Perhaps that was simply a result of lying full-out on a bed—naked as a loon—waiting for her lover to join her and feeling no shame at all. (Well, such a small amount of shame that it was practically nil.) What a marvelous concept.

Finished with his task, the ribbon tied in a surprisingly adept bow, he approached the side of the bed where she waited. Instead of joining her, he stood surveying her, one fisted hand on his hip, the other cupped around his generous, aroused anatomy.

"Thea." Actually, he stood *grinning* down at her. Incongruous, given the swelling surrounding his right eye, the deepening bruises on his ribs.

Her heart gave a flutter at the look of mischief his misshapen smile somehow expressed, one side pulled up slightly thanks to the stretched skin of his cheek.

"Aye?" She shifted atop the coverlet. Had she done it wrong? Did he want her back at the edge of the mattress so he could keep standing?

Drat everything to Dartmoor. How she wanted to feel his weight on her again, to touch the silky covering of hair adorning his chest.

His chest. If one discounted the discoloration, his torso was a work of art.

Merciful God in heaven. How blessed she felt, for never in her imaginings had she known such an amazing sight could exist: her benefactor, strong and manly; at once both powerful and yet protective. Saliva began to accumulate in her mouth the longer he stood there, and she wanted nothing more than to run her hands over his impressive physique. The sight of him waiting calmly next to the bed—ready to be intimate with *her*—sparked sensations in her breasts, belly and loins as all three places tingled and yearned for his touch.

But that was all he did—waited.

So she *had* mucked things up?

"My apologies." She pushed to sitting and swung her feet toward the floor. Unfulfilled urges made her a tad cranky else she never would have huffed, "Would you have said something, I wouldn't have changed positions—"

Cutting off her efforts, he swept her into his arms and lay down—with her solidly against him. With his body *beneath* hers. "You're p-perfect."

His words were muffled as he flipped her over and arranged her directly atop his limbs—face up. Shocking notion, that.

Bombarded with stimulation from all sides, it was all she could do not to swoon. His strong, muscular frame supported her posterior, the backs of her thighs, her spine and shoulders—her suddenly flexing and twitchy bum.

But her sensitized bottom wasn't where her attention stayed, not when she looked up. Where before her eyes, in the giant mirror's reflection, she saw herself—*stark naked*—for the first time.

Thea started to sweat.

Ladies, even gently bred females without an official "Lady" preceding their name, were taught never to look at themselves unclad. One learned early and well that *skin* was akin to *sin*.

One might bathe, might change clothing two or three times a day, might do all manner of intimate or necessary tasks to their person, and all without *ever* forgoing modesty. Only loose and fast women reveled in lewdness, in the lush sight of exposed limbs and blatantly revealed areas in between.

"Oh my." She had just made a staggering, and somehow satisfying discovery—fast and loose must also equate with fun and lusty because gazing at herself in all her slender splendor brought only positive feelings to the fore.

A sound of supreme something—excitement or pleasure, maybe—came from his throat when Lord Tremayne slid both his hands up her ribs to the under swell of her breasts. A similar sound came from hers when he dragged first one thumb and then the other over each nipple.

As though the desire battering her insides were happening to a stranger—the one in the mirror, perhaps—she saw her legs shift restlessly, felt the answering nudge of his erection.

Peering over her shoulder, he caught her reflected gaze overhead.

"Thea." It was sighed, giving her but a moment's warning before he extended one muscled forearm down her stomach to settle his hand just over her abdomen, fingers spread wide at the border where pale skin met dark curls.

Could one expire from desire? The sight of his hand, deliberately paused in such a place, was so forbidden, so arousing.

"Shall I—" She swallowed hard, her hips rocking ever so slightly, answering the thrilling call of his trespassing fingertips. "Turn around?"

How she wanted to.

Wanted to bury her lips against his neck, hide from the brazen female staring down at her, the pointy-tipped breasts being massaged and plumped by one strong, brown-fingered hand, the feminine length of leg pressed securely to hair-dusted thigh muscles.

Who was the lush wanton staring back at her? That woman in the mirror—she was a stranger. One Thea wanted to know better. And after only days in his company...

The man at her back made her feel things, see things, differently than ever before. His broad hand kneaded her left breast, then he widened his fingers, placing his thumb on one nipple while stretching his pinky over to the other. He pressed down, just enough to make her gasp.

"Please." It was a plea this time. "Let me face you."

His hot breath brushing a "Nay" across her ear was all the answer he gave. Well, that and his other hand moving lower, fingertips probing, parting—

"Bless me to Middlesex." Her eyelids squeezed shut; she didn't need to see, only to feel. The drift of one lone fingertip delving, venturing deeper, finding and then gathering moisture... The deliberate glide of that same finger, back up and over... over...around...

"*That's* where your tongue—last night—" She garbled to a stop when her pelvis jerked away from the soft invasion. Then jerked right back for more.

"It is." His tone was as tantalizing as his touch.

"Feels, um..." Her abdomen convulsed. "Ah—"

"Intense?" She swore he almost laughed and

couldn't help but peek, that naughty, indulgent mirror drawing her gaze like a patch of sunlight did a lazing cat, staring at the place where her thighs spread wide, thanks to her feet propped on either side of his powerful legs. Focusing on where his fingertip circled and petted and coaxed...

Her internal muscles wanted him to return. She wanted his body surrounding hers, her loins surrounding him, needed him plunging inside again where she could feel him deeper than she had anyone before.

She tried to roll over and tell him, but he stopped her with one arm across her waist.

He kissed her shoulder until she relaxed, sank back on him. "Hmm-mmm," he complimented wordlessly and kept trailing his mouth toward her neck, unhurried, sensual applications of his lips that beckoned her to leave everything up to him.

True relaxation was impossible. Given how his fingers continued their advance and retreat over that part of her that grew at turns tighter and acutely sensitive blossoming into something soft and receptive. Over and over he rubbed and stroked her to whimpering abandon, inciting the exquisite, unbearable pressure to build, always halting or changing the tenor of his strokes before she jumped from that dashed cliff her body sensed loomed closer and higher.

"Tremayne," she cried at last, frustrated, eager, so wrung out from walking the tightrope his fingers pulled and swung at will that her mind finally gave up. And she gave in to begging. "Lord Tremayne, *please*. What—"

Only then did he loosen his hold on her waist, halt the torture between her legs.

"Why did you sto— *Ah!*"

Before she knew what he was about, he curved both hands under her arms and hefted her higher.

The new position angled her head awkwardly toward the mattress, and it was too much effort to raise it. Too easy to concentrate on sensations instead of sight. On his arm sliding between their bodies, fumbling for a second, then firming as he positioned his erection at her entrance.

"Like *this*?" At the first nudge of his penis, her confusion cleared and she grasped the previously foreign concept. Still... "It's possible? From this direction?"

But already, her feet were moving over the mattress to give her more control, her abdomen pressing down, pushing her lady bits against the crown of his hard flesh. Her hips twisting and tilting to accommodate the silky glide of his staff pushing into her, wedging itself more securely inside.

"Oh...my." The sensations he wrought within her majestic. Unreal.

It was being split apart and made whole all at once. It was terrible, aching pain and incredible, awesome pleasure.

It was rainbows bursting across her closed eyelids and storm clouds gathering strength.

It was so good and so different and— "Wicked or not, I want to see."

When she tried to raise her head, her neck protested. Then his hand was there, his palm cradling her nape, his fingers supporting her skull. It was the sight of their heads, close together, both staring above, at each other...

It was his other hand reaching past her stomach, fingers splaying around his thrusting shaft, the heel of his palm digging into her, finding *that spot* and riding it...

Her pelvis vibrating beneath his touch, her feminine muscles clamped on for the ride of their life...

And it was her body balancing between restraint and release, hovering between power and weakness...

Her mouth forming a breathy string of high-pitched sounds, encouraged by his deep-throated murmurs...

And finally, shockingly, it was her loins winding into a coil of painful passion, so strong that when the crest finally came, it burst on a wave of wet release, a visible shower of—of—of, she didn't know what, but one that had his fingers flying swiftly over her intimate flesh, had him groaning approval and praise with barely discernible words, the only thing she had the presence of mind to comprehend, the husked, "You're a d-delight," which was more than enough.

She gasped, strove for breath.

Sweating. Crying. Heaving as air and delight

coalesced and bathed her insides as surely as her body had bathed his fingers.

His renewed thrusting and swirling touch made it clear that the rush of dampness she'd found so startling—and embarrassing, by the only part of her that wasn't reveling in the glory he'd brought her to —was something *he* certainly reveled in.

Just when she thought it was over, that she was descending into the replete and utter bliss he'd first taught her last night, that mayhap she could catch her breath, it began again—right beneath his dancing fingertips...

An urge.

A need that was more. Fierce. Nearly unbearable. "I cannot—"

"Aye." He used the hand supporting her head to bring her face to his. "You can."

His lips ravaged hers, his mouth taking possession in a manner more demanding than anything that had come before.

What a treasure!

Daniel couldn't believe the unrestrained passion in the slight package writhing over him.

She wasn't experienced enough to hide her responses; wasn't jaded enough to fake them. No mistaking that sweet, sweet flood of her climax, proof their bodies spoke the same language.

Knowing beyond a doubt he could give her this —carnal pleasure, a true appreciation of herself as a vibrant, sexual being—was one of the greatest gifts Daniel had ever received.

Giving to his precious Thea made it clear how he'd reduced sex to habit, done it by rote for too long, going through the motions without any feeling at all. For he'd never been more pleased by pleasing a lover more.

Never been more thrilled than when she splintered in his arms—under his command, around his cock.

And now—the taste of her honeyed mouth? The reciprocal surge of her tongue stroking his?

Her response lent steel to his shaft, fluidity to his strumming fingers...

Her Venus mound bloomed again.

She was close. He knew it. And she was scared. Shaking again.

Pushing his tongue from her and whimpering, "I can't. Not—"

Her body thought otherwise. He wasn't even moving his hand now. Wasn't pumping his cock into her. Nay, despite her initial hesitation, Thea's inborn instincts had taken over.

Now she was rocking into him, swiveling her hips frantically, her tiny fists clenched, nails dug into his wrists, keeping his fingers firmly on her.

Her primal keen blessed his ears as her responsive flesh engorged, jerked, and dampened his fingers yet again as her sheath rippled along his shaft.

Only then did he release his control and

surrender to his own climax, his essence jetting out in time with her inner constrictions, her near-shouted pants of, "Intense. Aye. *Intense.*"

Scant minutes later, just when he'd thought she'd drifted off, Daniel occupying himself with the simple act of holding her, she surprised him by rolling to her side and fixing her gaze on his. "You've rendered me speechless. 'Intense' is all I can offer."

His smile told her it was enough.

"Who's Cyclops?"

The unexpected question confounded the truth right out of his mouth. "My dog."

"Your dog?" She digested that for a moment. One elegant eyebrow arched in a show of pique, but her voice was only curious when she asked, "And I remind you of him?"

"What?"

"You said earlier I was just like Cyclops."

"Oh." Blast it. Had he? He loved the ugly, dribble-drizzling mongrel but wasn't sure sharing that would get him out of the doghouse or not. Hard to shrug lying down, but he made the attempt. "Rescued him. That's all."

"Hmmm." The eyebrow lowered, the lush lower lip pouted out, and Daniel was afraid he was about to be severely taken to task.

"I never knew," she began, suddenly shy, "there could be such tangible evidence of passion. Both before...and at the culmination."

He'd heard tell of it but doubted. Until now.

Until her glorious release. Praying he didn't butcher it, Daniel said, "You were, *are*...beau...tiful."

That shy smile blossomed wide and she snuggled against him once more. For about thirty seconds. Then she popped up to one elbow. "Did you know—Mrs. Samuels made peach cobbler earlier."

So he was forgiven for comparing her to his dog?

"*Peach. Cobbler.*" Thea repeated as though the very concept was akin to flying to the moon. Perhaps, to her, it was. After all, fresh fruit was a rarity for most. "I didn't smell it on the tray she brought. Dare we race to the kitchen? Winner claims the biggest piece?"

Race a mistress to the kitchen?

After the most *intense* sexual experience of his life?

Daniel considered the time. He considered all he had to do the next day. He considered his empty bed at home. "By all means."

THEA WOKE ALONE.

Warm and snug beneath the thick coverlet in her rose-adorned room, her face and the one arm that extended beyond chilled from the morning air. Sufficient light streamed from behind the curtains, telling her morning was well underway.

Regrettably, she had no recollection of Lord Tremayne's departure. She did, however, possess the sated, sore and sublime sensations of a well-loved woman.

Even better (or possibly not *better*; how could *anything* be better than how her body felt at this precise moment?), she had the memory of sharing peach cobbler in the deserted and dark kitchen, of feeding each other, of his mock complaint over *where* was her reply to his last missive?

"For I long t-to read *your* p-poetry." He'd laughed when she stuffed the last of her cinnamon-spiced bite in his mouth, giving him no time to swallow before she was kissing him, and he her. Wiping crumbs off his lips as he swept her into his arms and carried her up to her room, to her bed, where he lay down and pulled her against him, cuddling her close until Thea drifted off...

Only to wake this morning with a smile on her face. One that faltered when she sat up to be confronted yet again with her dress, laid out over one of the chairs in the corner. Dear Mrs. Samuels— the woman was a marvel. She must've snatched it from the dressing room floor and cleaned it during the night because the hem was clear of mud, the skirt freshly pressed. If wearing the same thing again didn't thrill Thea to the core, then the clean under- things stretched out beside it certainly did.

She pushed back the covers and braved the cool air, feet hitting the floor and stretching against the rug, reluctant to cross cold wood over to—

"What's this?" Stacked boxes on the circular table obliterated any reluctance and she fairly bounced across the room, where she paused. Savored. *Gifts.*

Drawing out the anticipation, she inspected the boon. There were four in all, ranging from one that nearly covered the entire table, to three smaller ones atop. Simple boxes, devoid of any wrapping save soft green bows tied around each.

Heart hammering, she watched as her arm reached out to caress one satin bow. The delicate fabric yielded beneath her touch. Her stomach dipped. Had she ever been this happy? Felt this secure?

For a certainty, not since her mother was alive.

Unsure where to start, she chose the second-largest box, and in moments stared, to the accompaniment of her astonished gasp, at a pair of quality half-boots. Made of dark leather and lacing up the front, they were the most fashionable boots she'd seen since childhood. New stockings were rolled and tucked inside. As though seeing another perform the actions, her chilled feet were tucked inside the stockings and then the boots in a flash, toes turning toasty.

Moving the box aside, she heard something clank. "More?" She riffled through the paper. "Oh, Tremayne..."

Shock nearly held her immobile as she spied the metal and wood pattens he'd thought to include, ready to be attached to the bottoms of her new boots any time rain made sludge out of the roads.

Blinking back amazement, she numbly opened

the largest box which yielded a lined cloak. A stunning, hooded garment *with a matching pelisse*. Fairies to Flintshire, she must be in a magical land herself, for surely she would sprout wings and fly. As she tugged on first the pelisse and then the cloak, she doubted her feet would ever return to earth.

The sleeves were only slightly too long, she realized, as she sat there cozily wrapped, staring down at her booted toes, all manner of delight and disbelief coiling through her.

Not to be forgotten, the smallest two boxes seemed to dance on the table, drawing her gaze.

"What else could he have sent?" Saving the smallest for last, she retrieved the remaining box. "He's already done so much."

Reverent fingers slowly untied the bow and lifted the lid. "Gloves!"

Thrusting her hands inside, she closed her eyes. The supple leather and fur lining stole her breath as surely as her protector had stolen her wits. *Dorothea, he's surely secured you now, bought and paid for.*

Trouble was, she didn't seem to mind. Not any longer.

After basking a few seconds more in her newly reduced and wondrous "lowered" status (ironic, as she'd never felt her spirits soar higher), she roused herself to open her eyes and her remaining gift.

Which contained an unmarked jar.

What commanded the largest smile yet, as she sat at her table bundled to the gills in her new winter finery, and lifted out the jar, was the folded square of paper that resided beneath. Setting it aside, still folded, she unscrewed the lid and a familiar, spicy-sweet scent greeted her.

Lord Tremayne's fragrance? She sniffed again. Nay, the crisp outdoors was missing, but it still smelled like him. Why send her—

"Read the note, you ninny."

Dearest Thea,

I trust you'll find these items useful, especially the lotion. Put it on your wrist and arm and I can promise the bruises will fade in no time. As to the other items, if anything does not fit or is not to your liking—

"Not to my liking? Has he windmills in his upper garret?" She wiggled one hand free of the fur-lined gloves to stroke bare fingers over the soft leather of the cloak. "Indeed, I like very much."

Pulling off the second glove as though it was the most precious of Meissen porcelains, she pulled up one long arm of the pelisse and rubbed the cream on one wrist. Whether the bruises disappeared or not, knowing she smelled vaguely like him made her old injuries vanish into the ether.

She inhaled, the scent of him in her lungs taking her back to taking him in her body, when he—

"Thea," she said tartly, "stop thinking of last night. Read on, missy."

Oh, but 'twas difficult when every shift of her legs brought to mind new sensations from last night.

Grinning like a goofy goat, she slid her fingers back into the gloves and picked up his note.

...not to your liking, I trust you'll let me know so I can provide something you prefer.

Now, woman, make haste—if you're reading this, then Swift John is waiting for my promised reply.

I do believe there's the matter of a poem you're supposed to share?

Tremayne

PS. I found much pleasure in our evening together. Thank you.

In only as much time as it took to remove the gloves, ready the quill, and add a postscript (or two) to the letter she'd composed yesterday morning, she sent Buttons on his way. But only after asking for clarification first:

"Swift John?" she queried the footman. "I thought your name was Buttons."

"It's actually James, ma'am. But my brother and me—we're twins, you recall? *He's* John."

"Which explains naught. How do you then come by Swift John?" And why did Lord Tremayne not simply call him James or Buttons?

The servant gave her an unrepentant grin. "On account of when we tried to snaffle his lordship's pocket watch, I'm the one who ran the fastest. My brother, John? Now he got hisself caught."

"You attempted to steal from Lord Tremayne?"

Buttons rocked back on his heels and gave every appearance of one who loved divulging this particular tale. "We did indeed. Only he wasn't his lordship back then. Nine, we were, and not particularly adept at the trade but hungry after havin' just lost our folks to the fever."

"Oh, James..." Just imagining two boys, so young, alone and grieving—

"Don't go worrying on about us, Miss H. His lordship's a real square cove. We couldn't have picked a better pigeon to try an' pluck—though we were the ones caught. After chasin' down my brother, Lord Tremayne stood in the street holding tight to John till he finally caught sight of me. Told us we could keep stealing and like as stretch for our efforts, or we could come with him and do honest work for food and pay without ever having to worry about a noose around our necks." His chest puffed out. "An' I've been *Swift* John to him ever since."

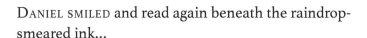

DANIEL SMILED and read again beneath the raindrop-smeared ink...

Drip. Drip. Drip it goes.
All day long, it grows...
The pile, the dripping,

Gluey, sticky pile...from his nose.

A sonnet (or is it an ode?) dedicated to Mr. Freshley of the Dripping Nose.

Thea (who will hurriedly blow hers and hope she's not given you a dislike for her magical quill—or her taste in literature)

P.S. The cloak, pelisse, gloves and boots are <u>lovely</u>. And though the sleeves are a fraction long (which I only confess because you'll see this for yourself since I plan to wear my new garments henceforth when I leave the house), I vow your gifts are <u>perfect</u>.

Perfect! Though you are dreadfully spoiling me, I fear, I quite refuse to give them up. Thank you a thousand times over.

P.S. Again. Bruise Fading Cream? What a concept for a pugilist. Are you secretly an apothecary? Or have one in your employ? I adore how it smells on you and will gratefully slather it on my arms. Thank you, kind sir!

P.S. III. I cannot express enough my appreciation to you for sending Buttons to join our household. Though I feel horribly overindulged, I will cherish his presence nevertheless (and perhaps request he give me directional lessons with all due speed).

P.S. IV. I too found great pleasure in our coming together *last night. (My face is about to flame at how I'm putting this to paper, but may I reiterate, <u>Great</u> Pleasure?)*

———————❖———————

...I'd much rather slather it on for you...

...I said you were too refined to be considered any sort of tavern wench? Another error in judgment it appears. Thank you for pointing it out, as I am one who can appreciate the fine, enthusiastic qualities a tavern wench (or in point of fact, my lovely mistress) might show when we're together and the bawdy sense of humor she might exhibit, and share, when we're apart.

As to your ode-worthy companion, I do hope you provided the remarkable, rememberable Mr. Freshley with a handkerchief?

———————❖———————

Alas, no. The grizzled Mr. Freshley would have scratched me ere I tried. He was the neighbor's cat, you see. I wanted to be friends, but he had differing definitions of friendship. (If I approached without a fish head or bird in hand, he wanted nothing to do with me.) 'Twas a true pity. Would you care to know what I penned to commemorate my first scratch?

———————❖———————

I shall be turning blue from lack of air until you share.

(Remarkable coincidence, that; it rhymed without effort —and 'tis obvious, eh?)

Once again, after sending Swift John off with his response, Daniel returned his attention to the areas Wylde wanted him to cover at the committee meeting. He'd put this off for days and could no longer justify avoiding it.

Trying to keep an open mind, because if his throat tensed along with his thoughts, he'd never get the words out, he applied himself to succinctly rewriting each salient point and then practicing the words ad nauseam—both in his head and out loud —until he deemed himself ready to move on to the next one.

With every phrase he committed to memory— phrases absent of pesky letters and sounds—he tried not to think of the other meeting he'd miss, the one he'd longingly thought to arrive right as it began and remain near the door, if only to catch a smattering of the brilliance that was Mr. Taft.

Mr. H. B. Taft, a gentleman Daniel had yearned to hear speak for years who was making a single London appearance. 'Twas no hope for it now; both events were scheduled for the same afternoon.

Disappointed anew, a heartfelt sigh shuddered from his lungs. He reminded himself of the good he was doing for his friend, if not for London.

Hell, poor Wylde had to have been desperate to

ask *Daniel* to help him out; any words out of his mouth were bound to be a cheap bargain. But by God, he'd give the man his pennyworth.

For upon taking the time to really study what all Wylde had prepared, Daniel had experienced a major change of heart. Once he realized the earnest passion in the arguments presented, and recalled the primary reason why his friend cared so much, Daniel was determined to do his best.

After all, if any man had cause to see an organized police roaming the London metropolis, it was surely Wylde.

My dear Lord Tremayne, you may not be so quick to condemn your own literary attempts once you read more of mine.

> *Mr. Freshley, pussy so fine*
> *Why on my arm must you dine?*
> *With teeth marks and hisses and scratches galore*
> *I must stop trying to befriend you. No, no,*
> *nevermore!*

Before you ask, I regret to admit we never made nice. He was a rotten mouser; I think I became better at it than he. I always suspected the (is it too indelicate of me to say "snot"? I fear it might be; please forgive me for asking) phlegm drip-drip-dripping from his nose might be the culprit. How can any feline be expected to sniff out prey if they're always sniffing snot? (Well, knock me over with a black cauldron, this pen does have its own way at times.)

I've only just recently forgiven Mr. Freshley for snacking on me when I was delivering fish heads. The skin he took from my arm was not given willingly, I assure you.

AFTER EXTENDING the latest message from his master, Buttons blotted the sweat from his temple with a weary-looking handkerchief. He didn't fare much better.

"You're flushed." Guilt crawled up Thea's throat. "We've been selfish, sending you hither and yon with scarce a moment to rest. Forgive—"

"Ma'am, if I may?" Buttons interrupted, stuffing the handkerchief deep in a pocket.

"Certainly."

"'Tis no hardship, I promise you. Me an' John—the other servants too—why, we haven't seen his lordship this animated in years. Even ate luncheon at his desk and I know he's beyond eager for your next one." Buttons pointed to the note she held. "I'll go down an' see what Mrs. S has cooked up this afternoon and grab me a quencher while you pen him back, eh? Be ready to run back to his lordship's in a trice."

The enthusiastic, sweating footman was off, racing down the stairs, leaving Thea to marvel at the fortune Fate had dropped in her lap and excited to read the latest missive Buttons had dropped in her hand.

Trust me, something as simple as a four-letter word, be it snot or any number of others, will not offend. In fact, I count myself honored that you feel at sufficient ease to talk thus with me. May it always be so.

Although once the question was posed, my mind would not rest until I'd applied it sufficiently, ascertaining what other possibilities you might have considered: snuffles, sniffles, sniveling...hmm, are you familiar with Captain Grose's Dictionary of The Vulgar Tongue? I proudly own a useless copy and took the time to peruse its pages. Tell me what you make of this:

TO SNIVEL. To cry, to throw the snot or snivel about. Sniveling; crying. A sniveling fellow; one that whines or complains.

TO SNOACH. To speak through the nose, to snuffle.

I trust you could come up with a rhyme or two that would work companionably with snoach. (Does anyone ever—in actuality—use that word?) Although since first reading about your dear Mr. Freshley, I do have it in my head that he's a snivler (aye, I just coined that one myself). Do you not agree? "To throw the snot or snivel about"—does that not describe your fiendish feline foe?

Now tell me more about your mousing talents. On that, I am aghast with curiosity.

EARLY THAT AFTERNOON, her written reply arrived. Only instead of regaling him with the most welcome and anticipated jovial rehash of her mouse-catching escapades, it contained one simple paragraph.

A simple paragraph with a relatively simple suggestion.

One that struck the fear of God into his heart.

Snoach! How could I have gotten on so admirably with such a lack in my vocabulary? You are quite right. Mr. Freshley was definitely a snoaching snivler! How could I not have seen that on my own? Perhaps, when next we meet, we should apply ourselves to joint compositionary efforts?

Pen some lyrical odes together?

What the devil?

Together?

His eyeballs burned as the syllables threatened to detonate in his brain, explode in his misbegotten mouth.

Oh Gad.

What was he doing? Thinking? *Saying?*

Idling his day away—flirting? And with *words*?

Now his new mistress wanted to write poetry—together? In *person*?

As though a serpent had just sunk fangs in his arse, Daniel bounded from the chair. The back smashed into the window behind him, shattering glass.

His canine's howl of surprise couldn't drown out the incriminating crash.

But the whining dog scampering toward the door and the singing shards decorating his floor were nothing compared to the black blanket of dread that swooped over him. Enshrouded him. Pressed him down, back into the righted chair, hands between his knees, head bowed.

Pray God, what have I done?

Forged a friendship on a lie? Wiled away hours, if not days pretending an interest in something that could never be. Damn him! Damn his mind for veering on to this blasted path. Damn his heart for jumping in head over heels. But most of all, damn his goddamn mouth!

SOME TWO HOURS LATER, after the glass had been cleared and the vacant window area boarded over, Daniel realized he was *still* staring into space, conjuring visions of Thea occupying his ornate bed upstairs, her hair splayed over his pillow, her body sprawled over *his*. By damn, he wanted to howl like Cyclops.

He was *not* some naïve Othello to be led around by *his* nose. Or by his frigger, by God.

What was he thinking? Imagining her occupying the London home he inhabited, the bed that had just paraded through his brain box, sporting images both lurid and lusty? In the very chamber where his revered grandfather had once slept, in the home he'd inherited from the venerable old man he'd not only wished was his father but the man who had taught him more about *being* a man than any other. About goodness and kindness. Sacrifice, even.

Distracted, feeling guilty because he *wasn't* feeling guilty at the idea of parading his paid paramour through these honored halls—and straight into that bedchamber—Daniel balled up the page that tormented him so and tossed it toward Cyclops, straight into the languorously extended paw that clamped over the missive.

"Woof!"

Instead of smiling at the dog's tail-thumping antics over "catching" such a treat—and with so little effort expended—Daniel found himself hard-pressed not to race his carriage to Thea's, toss her inside and return with her—upstairs. To his bed.

To make his vision a reality.

And that wouldn't do.

Wouldn't do at all.

No small amount of time later, a time during which he hadn't moved, not physically from his position, nor mentally from his fanciful musings, there came a knock upon his study door. A knock significantly subdued to indicate it didn't herald another letter from his mistress.

After rousing himself to retrieve the latest note— the one still languishing beneath Cy's paw—Daniel bade his servant to enter and quickly resumed his seat, smoothing out the page bearing the delicate penmanship and equally destructive suggestion. Joint compositionary efforts? Bah. He'd rather be roasted alive.

"This was just delivered, milord." Far different from when his brother bounded in bearing Thea's banter, John sedately placed a wax-sealed note upon the corner of his desk. "Buttons was curious about a reply? He swung back around just to check. I told him I'd bring it when—"

Daniel shook his head.

"I'll tell him nothin' yet." With an ill-disguised frown, the servant backed out.

Why did that look of disappointment make Daniel feel all manner of regret? What of it if his footman had lost the eager mien of a courting compatriot? Was disappointed his master was no longer flirting with a mistress?

"Goddamn waste of t-time," Daniel muttered with conviction as he reached for the just-delivered note, determined to convince himself.

"Woof!"

"So you want me to open it? T-to see who—" Upon noticing the formal presentation, the fancy wax-seal on thicker paper than he and Thea had been using, something tugged at the back of his mind. He broke the seal and looked straight at the bottom, identifying the sender. Dread reached down from his throat to seize his innards in a clawed grip.

Lord Tremayne—I trust you are well and not under the weather after yesterday's bout. I only write at the prompting of my son who <u>insists</u> something dreadful must have befallen you (ah, the anxieties of youth).

I myself claim the only thing that has befallen either of us is my memory. I must've mistook our appointment time. According to my wife, 'twould not be the first lapse.

Regardless, I remain at your convenience and heartily hope all is well.

Everson (& Thomas, who persists in looking over my shoulder)

Gads. How could he have forgotten? He never forgot appointments. Never. He didn't make enough to clutter his schedule, ergo, the ones he committed to he cared about keeping.

Ballocks! *His* should be seized in a clawed grip and twisted.

But what to do about Thea?

"D-dammit." One problem at a time.

All the self-castigation in the world couldn't make his pen fly fast enough.

Everson—

My sincerest apologies. Something unexpected occupied my morning and put me off my plans for the day. I do apologize, to both you and to Tom, for my unpardonable rudeness.

If you'll indulge me once more, I will be at your residence tomorrow morn at eleven. Nothing will keep me this time save your preference for another... You have only to specify.

Sincerely, Tremayne

Forty minutes later, still feeling like a horrid heel whose ballocks were in need of a good stomping, Daniel received Everson's reply acknowledging their newly set appointment.

"There. 'Tis settled till the morrow. Now to you, my d-dear."

So Thea wanted to compose poetry? Suitable punishment, that, after his deplorable disregard for his day's schedule.

Lesson learned—*Don't forsake your commitments because you're in rapture over your new mistress. In alt over pen-and-ink frivolity.*

Blazes. He felt like a total clodpate.

Definitely time to tone down, institute some distance between him and his new inamorata. Why, with the last one, what's-her-name, he routinely got by seeing her once a week, sometimes less. With

Thea, the thought of skipping *one day* without her company spiked a shaft of angst straight through him.

And that wouldn't do at all either.

So turning his nose up at their earlier literary whimsy and completely ignoring her suggestion—the absolute *last* thing he needed to do was whimwham with her over words—he wrote...

Thea—

I regret I cannot meet with you this eve; a prior commitment calls to me. However, I should like to make it up to you tomorrow afternoon or evening. Where may I escort you? Anywhere in London. Consider the city and its environs at your disposal. Where would you like to go? What would you like to do?

There. That should prove suitably penitent (for lying about having something else to do tonight) as he was, in essence, giving her free rein. Pray God, whatever she chose was not his undoing.

I hope you enjoy yourself this evening, that your commitment is a pleasant one.

Pertaining to the morrow, I thank you for the generous offer but I am quite content to entertain you here. Mrs.

Samuels is a fabulous cook; would you care to join me for dinner? What time may I look for you?

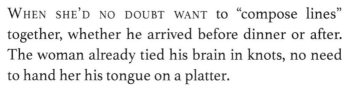

WHEN SHE'D NO DOUBT WANT to "compose lines" together, whether he arrived before dinner or after. The woman already tied his brain in knots, no need to hand her his tongue on a platter.

Especially where there was nothing to distract them save each other. An outing would provide a buffer. When he brought her home and they were alone, *that* would be the time to rush his fences and rush her up to bed.

Pen in hand, doubts hovering, he wrote:

Nay. I insist. It's beyond selfish of me to keep you stashed away.

Selfish, mayhap but smart.

Come now. Name your pleasure... A drive in Hyde Park? Perhaps a picnic?

Hell. With either, he'd be expected to chat. To converse. To reveal himself as a word-stumbling, bumbling idiot and that wouldn't do. Not with her. Never with her.

Gripping the pen tighter, he attempted to recover.

A drive in Hyde Park? Perhaps a picnic? Strike that. I
hear thunder rumbling near—

He didn't.

*so the ground will likely be too wet for an agreeable
outing.*

If it wasn't, he'd spit from here to Sussex to
ensure that it was.

Damn. Where could he take her? An outing
where *she*'d have a chance to sparkle and shine and
he could blend in and be unnoticeably mute? Where
she could visit with someone other than his stammering self? Somewhere he could keep his bone box
shut and just watch? Allow her presence to soothe
his soul without vocalizing his inadequacies. Where
he could simply sit and enjoy the enchanted bounty
that was Thea?

Needing ideas better than his own, he rang for
John and instructed him to bring up the latest round
of invitations. Everyone knew the "reclusive and
barbarian Lord Tremayne" wouldn't attend, but his
title ensured the blasted things kept pouring in.

When nothing remotely palatable presented
itself—a ball was out of the question, even one
where a man's mistress might attend; he'd plant a
facer on any bounder blighted enough to ask Thea
to stand up with him—Daniel requested the
morning papers he'd discarded earlier. There had to
be *something*.

Ten minutes later, he'd settled on the theater.

A nice, relatively safe option. The performance would entertain so he didn't have to. It'd be the carriage ride there and back and any intervals during. Did the theater even have rest intervals? He didn't remember. Wasn't sure he'd ever gone. But what did it matter?

Thea would love it and when they arrived back at her townhouse, he'd love her.

A bang-up solution all around. And if she started nattering about poetry in the carriage, he'd just kiss her quiet.

Daniel congratulated himself on his perfect plan.

He finished composing his missive and sent it off, feeling light in his chest. And heavy in his groin.

So it was with utter dismay that, shortly thereafter, he read her most unexpected response.

Nay. I do apologize for having to insist upon this, my lord, but I will not, I cannot attend the theater with you (no matter how much I might wish to).

Do you?

Do I what, my lord?

———————◗◦◖———————

"Oh, for God's sake." This conducting a love affair through letters had blossomed from asinine into absurd.

L-l-l-love? *Love* affair?

Forget his tongue, his head tripped over the thought.

Choosing to shoo away the unpalatable concept by stuffing it deep, deep into a dark corner of his soul where time would surely snuff it out so it never warranted further contemplation, Daniel gripped the pen hard enough to strangle. He had to, in order to still the sudden trembling in his fingers.

Printed so heavily the nib poked through the page in two places, he wrote:

Do you wish to attend the theater with me tomorrow night?

If "Aye", then why will you not agree? If "Nay"—

"If 'Nay', then I've half a mind to lock you into your b-bedchamber—and lock myself in there with you. Pun-punish us both."

If "Nay", then, for the love of God Almighty, woman, what <u>would</u> you like? What can I do <u>for you</u>?

And if, upon ordering John to deliver yet another missive, as daylight eased into dusk and limped straight into dark, Daniel salvaged his conscience by pressing an extra coin or two into his footman's palm, well then, he could be forgiven.

John or Swift John? Hell, he'd seen them both so many times today, he was no longer certain who stayed at his residence and who resided at Thea's.

"Owe you new shoes," he muttered as the man grabbed the folded letter with a grin so wide, Daniel exerted real effort to avoid wiping it clear off his servant's face—with his fist.

At least one of them was finding his new situation amusing.

THEA'S REPLY, when it came later that night, staggered him.

What can you do for me, you ask, astonishing me to the point my eyebrows ascend to my hairline?

Lest you forget, you spectacular man, you have already given me the world: A safe home, one that I'm not constantly defending against mice nor men. Plentiful food and wondrous hands to prepare it, so that my empty stomach no longer wakes me during the night.

You have given me so very much that I hesitate to trouble you for anything further.

Yet, you have requested so little from me in return. So

now that you have posed the question, I feel compelled to answer from the heart, with the same earnestness with which it was asked.

I would like to spend more time with you. For our time together to flow as my magic pen does across the pages you've seen fit to so generously provide.

I would like for the hesitance that often characterizes our in-person interactions to ease and the inviting, invigorating tone of our written correspondence to take its place. You make me laugh so easily, in person and on the page, yet I find, reluctantly I admit, that I do not know you at all.

How do you spend your days (other than getting beamed on the nose and clobbered on the ribs, if you will forgive my impertinence)?

What matters concern you? Matters of state, matters of your own holdings and responsibilities? Matters of family? I would listen to it all, if you would but share.

What things do you like? Rainy days by the fireside or walking in the sunshine? After-dinner port or evening brandy? Strolling in the countryside or shopping in the busy streets? Arm-scratching, nose-dribbling cats or rescuing playful, barking dogs?

Have you any personal interests? Any favorite pastimes or nonsensical enjoyments?

What do you dream of? (Whether you wish your nosy mistress would squelch her inquisitive nature and leave off pelting you or your life dreams...I wish to know them all.)

~~I wish to know whether you're married, possibly have children~~

That last, she'd crossed through so much that he had a devil of a time making it out.

In all honesty, I wish to know so many things about you, but I quite wonder whether you've continued to read this far.

Aye, I would <u>very much</u> treasure attending the theater with you (most anyplace, in fact).

But I simply cannot, my lord.

And please do not laugh at my reasoning. I don't claim to know how things are conducted in the upper reaches of society, but I assure you, I exaggerate not my situation. The bald truth is...

The reason why I cannot accompany you is...frankly...

Well, to be perfectly blunt, I haven't a thing to wear.

5

SQUINTING QUINT'S QUALITY QUIZZING GLASS

Squinting Quint's quality quizzing glass is queerish fine;
before he got it on Quarter Day,
the quaint, quaking man had been in quite a quandary
when queried to dance the quadrille!

Thomas Edward Everson, *Lyrical Lines for Education,*
Elocution and Entertainment, circa 1820s

THE NEXT MORNING, Thea nimbly ran her fingers over the keys of the pianoforte they'd found stashed away, along with a host of older, unused furnishings, in another bedroom upstairs. Mr. Samuels and Buttons had liberated the shrouded piece and shuffled things around so Thea and Mrs. Samuels could give the old instrument a thorough cleaning.

Those efforts had defined Thea's day after she'd sent off the final, unanswered note to Lord

Tremayne. Now, though, even the reality of the pianoforte failed to make her smile.

The sounds it made when she picked up speed weren't quite enough to make her cringe—but they were close.

The sun sliced in through the open window, promising a warmer—and drier—day than the preceding few. It was still early enough she wasn't yet worrying over what Lord Tremayne's response might be to her last missive, nor was she agonizing over why she hadn't she heard from him yet (not overly much, anyway). But it was late enough she was definitely wishing she'd added one more request to her brazen list of what all she wanted.

If she was going to pelt him with a plethora of requests, she might as well include everything.

A piano tuner. By Jove, she'd neglected to ask for a piano tuner.

She played a little harder, a little faster. A lot louder. And then she did cringe—*how could she?*

A new mistress didn't rail at and complain to her protector, not when things were going rather swimmingly, and not if she sought to retain her intimate position in his life. Which she did, oh, how she most definitely did.

The discordant notes that followed echoed her uncertain mood.

"Miss Thea!" Buttons burst through the open doorway. "Down...stairs..."

He was out of breath, both hands dangling at his

sides, neither extending a folded square in her direction.

So, no note, then.

Disappointed, apprehension growing at her no doubt off-putting forwardness, she tried to whip beautiful music out of the stubborn old pianoforte. (All she whipped were both their eardrums.)

Her fingers never breaking stride, she asked, "What is it? Something certainly has you in a dither."

"You're needed downstairs," he repeated in a more normal voice and she glanced up in time to see a secretive smile flash across his lips before he wiped it clear. "You have guests."

Her fingers fell from the keys. "Guests? Plural?"

"Aye."

"Who?" She reached the doorway but hung back, leery of venturing out into the unknown. What kind of guests visited the abode of a mistress—other than its master, who arrived most definitely *not* in the plural?

"Come and see." Buttons' posture urged her to hurry. "You won't be sorry."

Taking the trusted servant at his word, she sped down the hallway and flew down the stairs, only to come up short at the sight of Mrs. Samuels beaming at her.

"Get yourself settled and I'll bring them in." The woman stood in the entryway, all but blocking the closed front door. She pointed toward the morning room near the back of the residence. That particular room was airy and inviting, decorated in simplicity and pastels. (Not at all like the sumptuous squares of decadent debauchery of the entry and master bedchamber.) "Go on with ye now, can't keep them waiting."

Them? "Who?" Thea tried again.

But the bustling housekeeper had already slipped outside through the narrowest crack in the door. Thea heard her telling someone it would be but a moment.

"Ah, miss?"

Not yet to the morning room, Thea halted when Buttons spoke. "Aye?"

"You'll want to read this first." Winking, he tucked a familiar-looking square into her hand. "I'm goin' back out to help Samuels get the mare settled."

"The mare?" Thea's fingers trembled on the unopened note.

"Callisto, ma'am."

Callisto? What manner of lord named a mare after one of Jupiter's moons?

"His lordship sent her an' a small carriage 'round too."

A mare. And a carriage? When she'd half expected her *congé?*

Bemused, she quickly claimed a seat and unfolded the page, trying to give the appearance of a lady of leisure—one accustomed to receiving surprise guests—while inside, her heart set up a distinctly unsettled rhythm.

Forgive me, Dear Thea. I've been negligent, inexcusably so, forgetting to tell you that you have accounts arranged in your name at a number of establishments, that you are free to spend, within generous reason, to your heart's content, outfitting yourself and your home.

For today, I beg of you, my proud girl, work with Madame Véronique. She'll see you grandly clothed and I shall see you this evening. Be ready at 6 p.m.

Daniel

Daniel. His given name was Daniel.

And he hadn't taken offense at her requests. Hadn't taken her to task for the audacious listing of them. Had, in fact, responded with even more consideration, more generosity. He'd sent her a horse and carriage, and, more amazingly than an unexpected invitation to dine with their rotund Regent, signed it with his given name!

Thea had no time to savor the realization, not when "Madame Véronique Rousseau, exquisite dressmaker to London's elite" immediately presented upon her doorway.

A tall, handsome woman with mounds and mounds of brightly hennaed hair, Madame V, as she said "Meezes Hurwell" could call her, spoke with an unmistakable French accent. Unmistakably fake, Thea suspected, but the words were delivered with such arrogance, she doubted very few ever quibbled with anything the haughty "French" woman might want.

With entourage in tow, comprised of three assistants carrying boxes piled high, she swept inside as though she were a tornado that made no allowance for anything in its path. And tornado was a perfect comparison, for within a matter of seconds, Thea found herself surrounded by a profusion of books, patterns, bolts of colorful fabric and swatches of even more, lace, trims, edgings, ribbons, hats...the previously sedate morning room becoming a storm of productivity.

And that was only the first trip!

After the second round of all three bringing in yet more boxes, aided this time by Buttons whose arms were piled high as well, Thea's startled gaze flitted from girl to girl as they pulled forth dresses in various stages of completion, each more beautiful than the one before. Once the final box was emptied and the last dress swished softly into place atop the settee, Madame Véronique clapped her hands imperiously. "Come now, girlz. Yvette, clear zee floor. Josette, find a stool or crate for Meezes Hurwell to climb upon. Suzette, ready yourself to take zee notes." A snap. "My measuring tape!"

Trying not to laugh at the false accent or phony names proved surprisingly easy once the first dress was held up to Thea's form and she was shoved in front of the mirror Mrs. Samuels brought in. (Hard to giggle when one is gasping.)

Time passed in a haze, fittings and pinnings

interspersed with various pronouncements from Madame V...

"Zix p.m.? He expectz zee miracle!"

"Suzette, for the last stinking time, leave off making cow eyes at that footman!" (In her exasperation, as this was the third such warning, Madame V's accent took a tumble.)

"Tsk, tsk, Meezes Hurwell, you are a stick, a twig! Theez will never hang right! You are a weed, a—"

By now, Thea had heard enough mutterings and criticisms about her shortage of natural padding to vex even the most patient of saints. She might be down to only chemisette (a peach-colored silk, it should be noted) and bare feet, but in recent days, she'd finally learned to stand on them—and stand up for herself. "Madame V, I appreciate all the work you're doing on my behalf, but where my figure—or lack of one—is concerned stop comparing me to spindly vegetation! I vow, pretty dresses and unmentionables aside, if you don't harness your nettling opinions forthwith, I'll eject you all."

After that, the fittings continued much more silently, and if Suzette caught Thea's eye and gave a nod of approval that caused Thea to blush, then it was all for the better. Blonde and buxom and so very

English, Thea thought she might've stepped right off a dairy farm in a neighboring shire; there was *no* conceivable way that girl came from across the Channel. And if she had a fondness for Buttons? Well then, Thea liked her already.

"Six p.m.? Never!" The accent had been long discarded. "I'll never have it ready. 'Fit for a princess' he orders..." Madame V complained from her kneeling position near Thea's feet.

"Lord Tremayne?" Arms straight out, Thea had been forced away from the mirror and off the stool as the hem was checked and rechecked.

"Lower them. Aye, Tremayne." As though coming to a decision, Madame V left off fiddling with the hem and stood. "Yvette, ball up some cotton. I need to fill in the bodice."

Madame might have abandoned the accent but Thea wasn't ready to falsify her bosom. "I'm not sure—"

"I am." The woman was adamant. "If I had designed this for you from the beginning, 'twould not be necessary, but alas, he orders you clothed like a queen *for tonight* and I am left with altering what already exists. I positively cannot have one of *my* creations fitting so ill. You're not a scrawny scarecrow without a *hint* of curve"—at least she'd unbent that much in her assessment of Thea's form—"and it would do no credit to my reputation to have your dress hanging on you as though you were."

"Mum always said that all a girl needed was to pop out a babe or two and her bosom would plump out right nicely," Suzette said helpfully.

Madame tugged the neckline forward and Thea frowned at how much it gaped.

"I shall make a temporary fix," the dressmaker announced. "The padding, it will be removable, hmmm?"

She shoved the small, rounded wad of cotton Yvette handed her behind one side of the bodice and smoothed the fabric over it, then leaned back to evaluate. Stepping in front of the mirror, Thea had to admit the addition did help the dress flow across her figure better.

Behind her, Yvette confirmed the theory. "She's right, Sally Ann is. My sister done got poisoned by the groom's seed and she's grown two inches in the bosom already!"

"Poisoned?" Thea whispered, glancing toward Suzette. Madame had dropped to her knees again and was humming over the hem, a nice, calm tune that told Thea she much approved.

"'E got her with child," Suzette explained, "with no plans to claim her or the baby."

Not to be left out, Josette poked her head between them. "Well, my mum told me that after you suckle your first babe, the pair of 'em will be drooping an' saggin' down so far on your chest, you'll wish—"

"Josette! Zee lips—zey are to be shut!" Madame

V was back, the relaxed interlude over. "Hush zee mouth or I shall pin it shut with zee hammer!"

"A pin? Don't you mean *nail* it shut?" Suzette asked, and Thea laughed, earning a glare from the dressmaker and another round of grumpy fittings when the perfectionistic seamstress decided to start over by modifying an altogether different dress.

"IF YOU WANT this finished for tonight," Madame V gritted out some time later, "you best leave off talking and twitching!" She grumbled a curse, then seemed to realize this wasn't the best way to address a new customer. Stretching her lips into a semblance of a smile one might expect to find on a beached barracuda, she added, "Zee rest will be ready for zee fittings three days hence. I will ezpect you at zee shop during regular hours."

"At your shop?"

"*Wee*, Meezes Hurwell. Henceforth, you'll come to my place of business, in Leicester Square, for zee remainder. For even zee indomitable Lord Tremayne, I refuse to close shop for another full day. Further business will be conducted there, and that is *final!*"

"Yes, ma'am. Aye, aye."

"One could wish your arse had as much cheek as your mouth," Madame muttered beneath her breath, her head bent over a delicate seam she was taking apart.

Thea caught Suzette's gaze and the two shared another smile.

"One could," Thea said clearly, barely suppressing a laugh at the audible *rrrriiiippppp* that followed.

"DOES HE DO THIS A LOT—ORDER fittings?" Thea asked, the next time Lord Tremayne's name was mentioned, this time by one of the girls, who was complimenting his manly physique (to the titters of the other two, and the narrowed gaze of Madame). It had been in response to Thea's curiosity over the vast array they'd brought, which she was informed he'd had a hand in. "Make selections and choose fabrics and patterns?"

It seemed an odd occupation for the man she was coming to know.

"For his sister, he did," Madame answered distractedly, pinning in the sides so the dress didn't *hang like zee sack*. "Before she was married."

Before she was married.

Which still didn't tell Thea if *he* was...

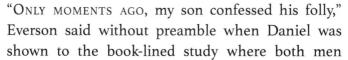

"ONLY MOMENTS AGO, my son confessed his folly," Everson said without preamble when Daniel was shown to the book-lined study where both men waited.

After nodding at the butler who pulled the door

shut after Daniel entered, Everson, he continued. "In his overzealousness, I regret Thomas badgered you unpardonably. Please be assured, Lord Tremayne, it will not happen again."

Everson's proclamation totally threw Daniel's carefully rehearsed opener out the window.

Twice he opened his mouth; twice he closed it. A heavy silence filled the air as they waited for him to respond. Tom snuck covert glances toward Daniel, his expression alternating between guilt and ill-concealed adoration. Everson looked at him steadily, confident that his son wasn't about to be raked over the coals any more than he'd apparently seen to.

The stalwart support in this family continued to astonish him.

Leaning his walking stick against the back of a heavy chair, Daniel caught each man's gaze with his own. "Aye. Well." He stalled, thinking swiftly. "I owe...both you fine gentlemen a sincere ap-p—" Dammit! "'Ology," he finished, trying not to curse aloud at the blunder.

All blasted morning he'd debated on how to proceed. Debated on whether to confess *his* badgered B's, destructive D's, and all-around abhorrence of public conversation. Well, ever since he'd dispatched John with the proper purse of coins and folded notes to ensure Ellie's most favored dressmaker's presence at Thea's.

Did he now accept Everson's apology and bow out? Escape home with none the wiser? Even though he was the one in the wrong (arriving a day late, being unpardonably rude)? Or did he go against everything instilled in him since earliest childhood and—

Tom made the decision for him. "L-l-l-lllord Tremayne, Fa-Father is rrrrrrrright-t-t-t, he is. I knew better than-than-than to ac-c-c-c-cost you but I-I—"

All it took to halt the eager and contrite youth was a wave of Daniel's hand.

When Tom fell silent, Everson nodded to his son. "That will be all, Thomas. You may—"

"No. P-please," Daniel said, determined to face his unmasking like the man he strived to be and not as the coward his father had made him. "Stay, Tom, please. I have words for you b-b-both."

He could see Everson's eyes narrowing, as though he suspected foul play was afoot, about to be brought down around his cherished son. Oh, to be that loved and protected!

The muscles in his neck clamped into a block. His next two attempts at speech were garbled beyond recognition. Damn.

Damn-damn! He would *not* let his body betray him again. Not now. Too much was at stake.

He might only face two men and not the several that loomed, but *these* were men whose opinions mattered. Whose respect he wanted to deserve. Needed to earn.

Those noddies in Wylde's committee? That was duty.

This? *This* was honor.

Daniel picked up the walking stick, determined for once to be "charmed" by his sister's incantated concoctions and, despite the fiery siege laying claim to his throat, he forged onward.

"Nay. Please—" Daniel tried to speak swiftly, to explain before he was tossed out on his ear. And for all that, taking longer than ever. "'T-tis not a trick or jest I pl-*play*."

He turned to Tom, his face as unguarded as he could make it. "You, T-Tom Everson, are the b-bravest man I have ever met. I regret I could not t-t-tell you the other night bu-but…"

Unable to face either of them the more he stumbled about, he clutched his walking stick and spoke to the ivory knob hidden beneath his fingers. "I was t-t-*taught* to hide it, t-t-to not speak—have the b-beatings to show for it." He smiled grimly and risked an upward look at Everson, only to find comprehension and compassion coming from that quarter.

Though he spoke to Tom, his next words were for the father. "I p-p-pray, should I ever b-b-b-be blessed with children, I can be as good a father as your own."

Making sure the youth knew he meant it, Daniel said what had been milling about his garret for days. "And, T-Tom, if you still have an interest in p-pounding me to a pulp in the ring, would b-b-be honored to work with you. But your father isn't—" *A bad hand*, he was about to say, but was overshadowed by Tom's response.

"Wwwww-*would* I!" The exuberant young man

started to rush forward but checked himself. "Cap-cap-capital! And I pr-prom-prom-ise, no one will-will-will hear from me." He indicated Daniel's head, then his own mouth. "'Tis your-your bus-in-in-ess."

"Nor I." Everson weighed in, coming forward to cover Daniel's hand, causing him to realize the strength of his hold was about to shatter the ivory. "And you have no idea how relieved I am, in some selfish ways, you understand." The man patted his hand once, then released him. "I always suspected you never liked me, just tolerated boxing with the big lout who never could learn any better."

"Never that," Daniel vowed, finding his hand gripped in a strong, comforting shake, almost as though Everson hugged his entire body with that simple touch of curved fingers and palm to palm. At least now he knew where Tom had learned that!

A nod of understanding and accord passed between the two men and their hands separated.

"Now," Everson began, after taking a deep, relaxing breath, one it seemed Daniel's lungs automatically echoed, "Thomas told me *what* he asked of you and that it had been done in a social setting. But he failed to tell me exactly *where* you two met—"

"'Twas-'twas at L-L-Lord P-P—"

"Hold up, Thomas." Everson cast a fond glance at his son, then caught Daniel's gaze. His lips curved in a gentle smile that spoke volumes. "Let's all sit, shall we? I think this may take a while."

Daniel laughed. He actually laughed.

And so the story came out between the two of

them, haltingly slow, furiously fast, in bits, starts, stops and stammers, but it came out. Gratifyingly, for once in his life, without a speck of aggravation.

It was simply a conversation that took a rather long time (a *really* long time), and that was just the way of it.

A pleasance he hadn't anticipated buffeted the day's exchange, the ease he experienced conversing with these two fine gentlemen nothing short of remarkable.

Positively remarkable.

At some point, after first taking refreshments and then lunch with them, talk naturally turned to Thomas and Daniel's difficulty. "I had a cousin who stammered as a boy," Everson explained. "He eventually grew out of it, but a physician his parents consulted made several recommendations..."

As Daniel idly listened, he couldn't help recall how the only physician he was ever paraded in front of wanted to slice out his tongue, sever off the nerves in his lips. Father had supported the notion and an all-out brawl ensued when one very determined ten-year-old made his escape. The sour taste that tarnished his saliva was too easily evoked and he swallowed hard. Bad memories best forgotten.

He renewed his interest in what Everson was saying. "...favorite suggestion was that he practice reciting word puzzles and poetry—"

The word *poetry* set off an unwanted visceral reaction. But instead of casting up his accounts and heading for the coast, Daniel made himself calmly inquire, "Word...puzzles. What are they?"

Everson nodded to Tom who quickly—and surprisingly—rattled off, with only a hitch or two:

Naked naughty Nancy natters on like a ninny-
hammer while knitting napkins for the nob's
nozzle.

There once was a man, not a priest,
who fancied for himself a fancy piece.
So he counted his coins
through his stiffening loins
till he could buy himself into her crease.

While Daniel chuckled, Everson frowned. "Thomas, what have I told you about the bawdy ones?"

Thomas assumed a glum expression. "Nnnn-not while-while Mum is home." Turning to Daniel, he brightened. "But-but they're grand fu-fu-funnn."

"Helpful, too," Everson put in. "We don't know if it's the cadence or song quality, but with practice, he's able to spew these out like a geyser. They've really helped with his regular speech too."

Helped his speech? Daniel couldn't fathom it, the poor lad. Evidently his expression gave him away.

Everson laughed so hard he choked. "Truly, my lord. You should have heard him before."

Nodding enthusiastically, Tom added, "But these are mmmmmy favorites, the p-peh-personal kind.

Roses are red. / My name is Thomas. / Follow my lead, / I'll be your compass. And one mmmy brother wrrrrote: Roses are red. / My name-na-name is Sir Henry. / There's no time to waste. / To the privy I make haste." He finished on a grin. "Now-now you try."

As though housed in a glacier, Daniel's mind froze. But Tom looked at him so expectantly, he pried his lips open, determined to give it a go. Only what came out was a disgruntled, "Don't like p-poetry."

Everson smiled, that indulgent, fatherly smile Daniel hadn't received in years, not since his beloved grandfather passed on. "Here now." He scooted his chair toward his desk and pulled a sheet and the ink toward him. "I'll jot down a few of the others and you can practice at home, hmmm?"

"Much obliged."

While Everson wrote and Daniel tried not to be embarrassed by his lack of participation, Tom entertained them with several more surprisingly competent recitations.

Buxom Betsy bouncily brings brimming buckets of butter to bossy, balding Bob in the big, bug-filled basement.

Roses are red,
The birds they do chirp,
the worms, they do squirm.
But they don't eat the dirt.

"They do, really, but-but couldn't get it to-to-to rhyme."

Daniel smiled encouragingly and Tom finished off with two more.

Roses are red.
Words can be fun.
No matter what people may think.
I am not dumb.

Touched, because Daniel had no doubt Tom's father had written that one for him at a very young age, he was hard-pressed to maintain his smile. That was, until Tom's rendition of:

Jane Jubilee jubilantly jiggles with joy when Jack Johnson, a jug-bitten jackanape, jumps over with jacks. Just jolly!

"Bravo." Daniel applauded.

"It may be jolly, son," Everson said, still writing, "but you're going to wear out his lordship's wattles."

"'Tis fine. And call me D-Daniel, both of you." Another deep, pray-I-don't-muck-this-up breath and he exhaled. Resting his arm along the back of the couch, attempting to appear completely casual, he announced, "All right. I'll give it a whirl. *Ahem-hem.*" How long could he stall? His neck already felt rawer than squealing bacon. "Roses are red. / My name is T-Tr-*Tre*mayne. / Think we've all lost our marbles. / *But* at least we're not lame."

"Good!" Tom practically cheered. "Do-do anotherrr."

"Here you go." Everson passed him the sheet. "Try the top one."

He read over the lines to himself: Dashing Delbert, with pockets so deep, diddles his days away, while pretty Patty ponders by the pond, pitching puny pennies to dog-paddling puppies.

Gads. I'll destroy it.

He didn't realize he'd said it out loud until Tom said, "You're among fr-fr-friends, mmmy lord. 'Tis part-part of the fff-ffun!"

Everson gave him a reassuring pat on the shoulder. "Take your time, Daniel. There's no censure here."

6

COUNTERFEIT CHARMS CHARM THE TRUTH

For they breathe truth that breathe their words in pain.

William Shakespeare, *King Richard II*

"*Exquisite.*"

The rasped compliment raised the fine hairs at Thea's nape. Lord Tremayne's voice was deeper tonight, more rugged—if that were possible.

She hadn't needed the words to know he was well pleased with her appearance. The sudden gleam in his eyes as he surveyed her when she came down the stairs told her clearly enough.

She was too aware of the late hour—significantly past six—and too aware of her changed appearance to meet his gaze for long and hers veered away to focus on the rail where she placed her gloved hand to steady herself as she descended. Watching her satin-covered fingers slide down the mahogany banister was much easier than contemplating the forceful presence below.

A quick, lash-veiled peek told her he looked remarkably handsome, if somewhat different. She couldn't quite identify why, but it must be his clothes. She'd never seen him attired so impeccably, in formal evening dress, everything ink black save for the snowy cravat and white silk stockings beneath his knee breeches. Even his waistcoat was black beneath the snug-fitting tailcoat. Her heart gave a distinct lurch when she glimpsed the strong thighs—and impressive parts between—shown to exquisite perfection by the absurdly tailored breeches (if there was an extra wrinkle of fabric to allow for movement, she couldn't discern it).

A few steps from the bottom, a self-conscious hand went to the back of her hair where "Suzette," upon asking Madame if she could remain (under the guise of reboxing everything they'd brought), had offered to weave in a feather or two.

"It's all the crack," she'd told Thea, unearthing two iridescent feathers that shone with the same inner fire her dress did. The dress Madame had finally settled on, a rich, shimmering sea-blue confection unlike anything Thea had ever seen, much less worn.

It was also, to her dismay, the one with the falsified bosom.

No drawers either! Just beautiful silk stockings

tied at her thighs. "Drawers will ruin the glide," Madame V had imperiously informed her.

Thea felt so very debauched, and he hadn't even touched her yet. Oh, but she was primed for it. For their entire night together, for how it would end. With them in her bed, skin on skin, hot, slick, sweating—

She gasped as her left foot slipped on the step.

Lord Tremayne jumped forward but she waved him back as she regained her footing, determined to make it to the bottom unscathed. "Silly me. Best I watch where I'm going."

Buttons and Mrs. Samuels had hovered about all evening, laughing with Sally Ann (who'd professed to preferring her real name over the fancy "Frenchy" one) while Thea quietly endured their attentions. They were all excited about her first night out with "his lordship", and though she portrayed the epitome of ladylike composure, inside she was a fluttery, flustered wreck.

The look he gave her when she reached the landing didn't help. Trembling, she allowed Lord Tremayne to tug her in front of the mirror.

Where had the servants gone? Just as his hands settled heavily on her shoulders, a startled glance told her they'd disappeared into the woodwork.

Leaving two of them very much alone. And she was *very* aware of his tall and powerful presence brushing up against her as he snared her gaze in the mirror.

At the picture of her low—dreadfully low—

neckline, Thea struggled to smile. Had she ever before exposed so much skin? (Discounting their mirrored encounters upstairs, that was.) The padded corset plumped up the swells of her breasts to the point they were actually visible. It was a miracle. And oh, mercy to Mercury, there was a hint, just a hint mind, of shadow between them.

What dismayed her most was how her *nipples* (she thought the word on a whisper) nearly promised to peep over the edge of the deeply rounded bodice if she so much as sneezed.

She noticed her reflected image quivering and resolutely locked her knees. Over her shoulder, Lord Tremayne captured her gaze. Above those piercing eyes of his, thick, coffee-colored hair was brushed back with careless abandon, tempting her fingers to muss it further. "You look extraordinarily handsome tonight, my lord."

He gave an abrupt nod. The hard line of his jaw firmed. "You...are a jewel."

The swelling had gone down, both eyes were blinkable, but the bruising looked bad, deep purpling surrounding one eye and part of his cheek.

"What of that cream, my lord? The one that fades bruises?" She *tsk*ed. "It doesn't seem to be working."

"Almost out," he told her with a forced smile.

His face must be paining him, poor man. Why he seemed so strained.

"Then I'll just run up and grab what you gave—"

Tightening his grip on her shoulders, he pointed to the cuckoo clock beside the mirror. "Later."

Which she surmised meant they really needed to be on their way. "Very well."

She watched the motion of his Adam's apple bob once after he nodded grimly, the flexing of his tight jaw, the strong column of his throat—

"You—you!" Thea spun in place, her fingertips going to his chin. *That's* what was different about him. Not his attire at all. Not just the reduced swelling, but his *face*. "You shaved!" she accused, too surprised to temper her tone.

A muscle jumped in his cheek. He inclined his head.

Her eyes skimmed every feature as her fingertips echoed the same path, rubbing over the squared and stiff jaw, the discernible cheekbones, the strong jut of his chin. In truth, she was met with a countenance she could study for hours.

Every speck of skin his thoughtful action revealed lured her touch to linger. That is, until he frowned. "Thought you'd..."

Be pleased sounded in her head, conveyed by his eyes.

She wound one arm around his neck and pulled him down. Rising to her toes, she placed a deliberate kiss on the newly smooth skin. "I do like," she told him, leaning back and lowering her arm while keeping her gaze focused on his, "very much. Excessively much. It's just..." She darted a quick glance behind her and to the side, making sure the wood-work hadn't sprouted servants' ears.

When she remained silent, one of his dark brows lifted.

She spoke to his right earlobe. Good thing too, because she whispered so softly the confession was barely audible. "Just that I was never overly fond of men's beards until yours. I, ah, enjoyed the feel of it, *you*, ah...betweenmylegstheothernight."

His hearty laugh rewarded her courage. Taking her hand in his, he bowed over it. "It will grow."

And there he went, laughing at her again, *with* her now that she was laughing too. Gracious, but she'd become audacious since meeting him!

"La, sir," she said in her best "lady" voice, wishing she had a fan to playfully *thwack* on his arm, "how you love to mock me."

His expression was suitably stern when she garnered the courage to face him again. He straightened and Mr. Samuels magically appeared to open the door. Lord Tremayne took up his walking stick in one hand and extended his opposite arm to Thea as she retrieved her reticule. Nodding at the butler, he escorted her to the waiting carriage.

WHAT WAS WRONG?

The carriage ride, contrary to everything Thea expected, was fraught. Lord Tremayne hardly spoke. He barely nodded when she profusely thanked him for the lovely dress she now wore and the new wardrobe on order. Scarcely smiled when she shared about George and Charlotte, her efforts at first eradicating and then befriending the friendly rodents.

Only just acknowledged her laughing mention of poetry and how much fun she'd had bantering with him over noses and cranky cats. In fact, each topic seemed to pain him more than the one before until she was left confused and clueless, her fingers plucking at the reticule strings as she cast about for more to say, distraught that he might be tiring of her so soon.

But nay, he didn't seem disinterested, merely distracted, painfully so.

Once they left her neighborhood, the horses moved so slowly she thought they might be rolling backward. The seven—yes, seven—additional attempts at conversation she made were met with near grunts or hardly any response at all.

Night shrouded their meager progress, but the carriage's interior, unlike their last ride together, was well lit.

She knew he was pleased with her appearance. (He couldn't seem to take his eyes off her sham of a plumped-up bosom, which only made the scant pressure of the cotton feel like a ton, weighing on her conscience.) She knew he wanted to continue on because when she'd suggested they return home and stay in, some time after the silent ride commenced, he barked a nay.

The carriage rocked in place as one of the horses snorted. A huge sigh heaved from her lungs. She tried to look away, to focus anywhere except his newly revealed countenance but couldn't.

How could she ever have thought him unhandsome?

AS THOUGH AN OUT-OF-CONTROL bonfire threatened utter destruction, Daniel sensed all his efforts, all the relaxed time they'd spent together going up in smoke.

What a blighted evening!

At the townhouse, it had been all he could do to eke out his understated appreciation of Thea's glorious appearance.

His neck and jaw, throat and tongue, hell even his teeth and tonsils, were all weary to the point of exhaustion. He never should have done so much talking at Everson's. Not when he had plans this evening with Thea. But the afternoon had been so easy, once he'd moved past his initial reluctance, so... fun, dammit. Aye, *fun*.

Laughing over brandy and port, playing with words and letters, testing—and massacring—some of Tom's many tongue teasers. Once, when a maid brought in jelly-filled scones, all three of them had stuffed their mouths to overflowing and tried to sing Tom's Q list. *Squinting Quint's quality quizzing glass...*

Crumbs had spewed, coughs ensued, and the whole effort proved hilarious. He didn't know when he'd ever had such a rum time with someone he'd, for all intents and purposes, just met. He'd been himself, his habitual hesitance all but vanishing the longer he stayed in their presence.

Though he'd hurt at the time, he'd thought it a puny price to pay. Figured all would be fine in a trice.

Hardly!

For once he'd said his goodbyes, after making a boxing date with Everson and a lesson date with Tom, once he was alone and heading back home, it hit him: a pervasive tightness that seized his voice box and every muscle between his neck and his nose. Near excruciating pain that punished him—by gads, *him*—for talking too damn much. Talking!

Daniel assured himself a couple hours of rest would turn things around, soften the soreness and soothe the sting. Which was why he'd gladly agreed when Madame Véronique sent Swift John round with the message there was no plausible way Thea would be ready at six.

Seven, eight, midnight, Daniel didn't care, was happy to wait.

Maybe one of the remedies Tom had shared would help. He sent down to the kitchens for some precious ice, rubbed it all over his neck until he went numb. But when his flesh thawed, he was as sore as ever.

One remedy? Why not try them *all*?

So he sipped boiled water with honey, ate a lemon, lay on his bed and hung his head off the edge. Flipped over and let it hang from the other direction. Tried napping, gargling, and more stretching (who knew a man's tongue could extend so far?). And still, with each swallow, at the merest inclination of speech, agony screeched through his muscles.

Rest, we need to rest! they railed at him, embedding sabers and swords from the inside out, jagged blades that cut through tissue and bone until he stilled the urge, released and relaxed the fatigued muscles, silenced the desire to speak.

And sat mute, once again, like an idiotic imbecile.

Thea was aware of the change in him. Acutely aware, and she was baffled by it. He could feel her discomfort in every worn-out particle of his being. Twice he'd touched her in the carriage, once on her hands, once on her knee. Both times, she flashed him a grateful smile, as though saying, *It's all right.*

But it wasn't.

He couldn't lose her before they'd barely begun. And that dress! It bedamned and bedazzled. Befuddled his senses like—

"Season's in full swing, milord," the voice of his driver proclaimed at full volume. "Can't light a fart in this crush!"

"Roskins!" Daniel scraped out and banged on the roof as the woman beside him choked on a laugh. At least he hoped it was mirth and not disgust. Did the man forget 'twas not Louise he squired about?

As though he'd leaned close and lowered his voice, a muffled, "Beggin' your pardon, milord! Milord's lady friend, I meant no disrespect."

"None taken," Thea hollered back to his driver, "I assure you." Her lilting voice reassured *him*. Then stole his wits when she continued, "Had I a lucifer and the bodily urge, I might try it myself!"

Both men chuckled. And the carriage lurched ahead yet again.

Silence descended.

Weighed heavily.

Threatened to drown him.

Had air always been this thick? Or was his throat truly that swollen?

Long minutes later, when the horses had done nothing but inch forward a foot, Roskins yelled that there was no hope for it. He eased from the crush and took a sharp turn, coming to a complete stop (which was rather hard to discern, given how little they'd progressed). The man jumped down and opened the door, asking to confer with Lord Tremayne who gratefully stepped out at the unusual request.

Jointly, they moved toward the horses, out of earshot of the door, where Roskins continued. "The roads are clogged tighter than Prinny's privy, milord." He nodded toward his elevated seat. "Don't see it getting none better, either. Here's wot I'm thinking..." The man went on to offer several suggestions: take a longer route around, choose a different destination, try again another night.

Daniel latched on to the second option. "Any-where," he told his trusted driver, waving his arm and encompassing the whole of London. "Any p-p-pu-b-blic—"

He tripped over the words so bad he was surprised his tongue didn't flap out and flay them both. But Roskins had been with him a long time, knew how to interpret. "Another playhouse, milord, instead of the one we was aiming for? Will that do the trick?"

A nod and they each returned to their previous seats, Daniel only partially jealous of his driver's freedom up top, and alone.

How could he regret even one moment spent in her presence?

Easily, when he worried every one might be the last...

"Orreries!" exploded from his mouth as Roskins took off, the sudden forward motion jarring the occupants—and likewise his jaw. "Like orreries," he said more sedately in belated response to Thea's last note.

He wasn't yet ready to talk about family. (What would he do? Tell her his sister fancied herself a witch?) Neither was he comfortable with the notion of declaring what he dreamed about. (Did he even dream? Other than a good night's sleep and a fetching, accommodating mistress to help bring it about, Daniel didn't think he'd dreamed of much in years.) But he *could* tell her of his interests (if he could talk, that was).

Though the planetary models he'd loved since childhood had been popular for decades, they were definitely playtime fodder for the privileged class. Not something those untitled were often familiar with. Rather than assume she knew what he meant, he'd better explain. "They're pl-pl—" He licked his lips, tried again. "Pl-pl—"

Goddammit! The multiple, massacred efforts met his ears and he cringed. Even now, years later, there were times he had to remind himself a sharp birching wasn't on the other side of a hashed-up word.

Why in blazes had he decided to start answering her litany of questions *now*? When they were stuck in such a confined space? Where all he was left with was dreaded, deathly silence? Or...or he could kiss her senseless, toss her silky skirt over her head and plunder her pu—"'Lanetary miniatures!"

"Orreries," Thea responded in a delighted tone as though he hadn't just been flailing about in a stupid stew of his own making. "You have an interest in them? I'm familiar with them too, especially the inner workings."

Especially the inner workings?

She couldn't have stunned him more if she'd been a bolt of lightning. "Y' are?"

"Fancy trappings powered by clock mechanisms. That's the part I know about—the turning mechanism. I've seen a number of the smaller ones operating above clocks and a tabletop model or two"—she sounded wistful—"but I've never seen the larger, floor models."

"How?" It didn't seem to bother her—that he'd been reduced to monosyllables.

"My husba—" But she did seem to think better of that beginning because she immediately started over. "Mr. Hurwell operated a clock and watch service, you see."

Recognition snapped. *The Time Piece.*

That's why her name had sounded vaguely familiar when they'd been introduced. She'd been married to *that*? An older, slightly effeminate man who was bland nearly to the point of offense.

Daniel had stopped by the establishment twice, once to ask advice (which was given only grudgingly, even after the proffered coin was swiftly snatched away) and a second time to inquire whether the man would come to Daniel's residence and look at the broken arm on Uranus. *I don't make house calls*, he'd been dourly informed. *I'm a watchmaker, Lord Tremayne, not a physician.*

Damn. To think he'd been so close to her and had never known what a treasure the disagreeable Hurwell had stashed upstairs.

"My bosom!" Thea suddenly said, startling him away from the shadowy, crowded, ticking emporium he remembered and back to their brightly lit and now swiftly rolling carriage. "It's not, not this, well..." Her hands waved the air in front of her chest, fingers fluttering incriminatingly toward the creamy expanse of skin above the neckline. Skin he'd admired from the moment he'd seen her. The graceful neck, the beautiful, beckoning area below—

luscious skin he should have thought to adorn with a jewel.

Damn him again, why could he not seem to remember the most basic rules around her? Of course he owed her a bauble (after forgetting to outfit the woman, he likely owed her an entire jewelry store), but more than that, he wanted to see a stone he'd picked out, one that shone brilliantly and was cut to perfection, decorating the exquisite creature at his side.

In fact, he'd love to see her wearing jewels he'd ordered made up and nothing else.

But lack of a gemstone-encrusted necklace didn't appear to be the root of her dismay.

Thea stared at him, guilt in her eyes, a frown on her lips. "It's a complete deception. These..." She looked straight down and scowled at the gentle swells hinted at by the fitted dress. Then she looked back at him. "They're fake. Cotton. *Padded!*"

Mashing her lips together, she ruthlessly clasped her hands and stared off to the side. "Forgive me. I told Madame V 'twas not honest, to counterfeit my charms, but she wouldn't heed my opinions. Not on this. But there. I've told you now." She shot him a fast glance. "So why do I still feel as though we've tricked you? Lied about my form?"

I've seen your form, he wanted to tell her. *Have you heard a single complaint cross my lips?*

Other than her thinness, which was lessening by the day it seemed, he had no objection to anything about her. And yet, she was so obviously worried he might take offense. At something he had no doubt half the women who would be present tonight did as a matter of course.

It was charmingly sweet, Thea's earnestness. When had anyone so cared about warranting his good opinion?

He gave her a smile meant to reassure.

She still looked unconvinced.

"Thea." He had to waste time giving thought to his words. Preparing not to wince at the pain. "Know of men, re...spected ones, who enhance their own ana...tomy with filling."

For a moment he thought he'd have to try again. Then, simultaneously, her gaze dropped to his crotch and her cheeks flamed scarlet.

"You don't mean—" Lifting her lashes to face him, her blush deepened. "Oh, heavens to hades, you *do* mean. But you..."

Her arm stretched out between them as though she intended to test whether he did or didn't. Daniel would have let her. Would've been happy to have her hands on his body, but she snatched her arm back on a groan.

"I mean, you don't. *I know you don't.* Not that I would have any complaint if you did, you see, because I have tonight—have padded my bosom as I've just admitted. But I know you don't. Of course *you* don't. I've seen you up close, remember?"

By the last, her voice squeaked so high, it was a wonder the glass around the lantern didn't shatter.

Daniel couldn't help it.

He shoved across the carriage to sit next to her. Taking one gloved hand in his, he promptly placed it atop his non-enhanced masculine attributes.

"No...filling," he told her, gently curving her fingers around his hardening flesh. "Just you."

"Me?" The query was a soft sigh.

"Want of you enhances me," he eked out, hearing the harsh edge in his tone. "'T-tis all I need."

At the slip, he wanted to curse his blasted mouth. But she obliterated the urge the second she raised her head and meshed their lips.

He felt her smile against his mouth, couldn't help smiling in return.

He released his loose hold on the back of her hand—she caressed him now without any encouragement—and brought his fingers up to her shoulder, her neck, tilting her head as they jointly deepened the kiss, lips opening, tongues touching.

Like a spectacular display of pyrotechnics, desire exploded through him—

"Here we be, milord!" Roskins called out as the carriage bobbed to a halt. "The King's Theatre."

King's Theatre. The Royal Opera House. Where he had a private box, Daniel thought with supreme satisfaction. Where they could continue the kiss and, if they were both feeling bold, even deepen the intimacy...

"We don't have to stay," Thea breathed against his chin as they reluctantly broke apart. "Take me home and—"

"Nay. Show you off. Your new..." Dress. Gown. Attire. Gads, every word had an abhorred letter.

Easier to let it hang, especially when Roskins climbed down and opened the door. Especially when Thea playfully grumped, "If you insist," then jumped to the ground as though she were seven and a candy store awaited.

Aye. She deserved a fanciful night in her fancy new dress.

And Daniel? Well, he'd just count the minutes until it was time to take the blasted new dress *off* her.

To be continued.

Thanks for reading *Mistress in the Making, Book Two - LUSTY LETTERS*. If you have a chance to write a review, it's always appreciated. Reviews and word-of-mouth are two of the best things you can do for authors you enjoy.

Thea and Daniel both surprised me once they started exchanging notes. I had no idea Daniel had such a

sense of humor, nor that Thea, in all her relative inno-
cence, would be ready to respond in kind. I love it
when characters take on a life of their own and break
out of whatever personality box I thought they fit into.

Now that Daniel's ready to claim his mistress in public,
just how far will he go?

Turn the page for a look at *DARING DECLARATIONS*,
the final book in the *Mistress in the Making* Trilogy,
where these two finally get their Happily *Forever* After.

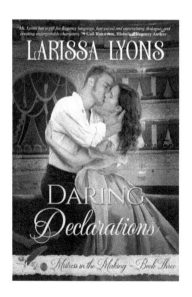

Chapter 1
Both Pleasure and Suffering

You who know what love is,
Ladies, see if I have it in my heart.

I have a feeling full of desire,
That now, is both pleasure and suffering...

Le Nozze di Figaro (The Marriage of Figaro), a popular
opera first performed in 1786

Thea was afraid to blink. *What if she missed
something?*

Bypassing the ticket booth, Lord Tremayne
conferred briefly with an employee before guiding
her straight through the foyer and up one of several
sweeping staircases.

Muted music indicated the performance was
well underway.

Mayhap arriving late was to their benefit? (No
one to see her gawking like a chicken.) Of a certainty,
the large rounded lobby they came out at on the
second level was only sparsely populated.

Lord Tremayne paused before entering either of
the two opposing corridors that she assumed led to
the private boxes, some costing in excess of two
thousand pounds per season she'd heard. That was a
vast sum more than most people earned in years,
abundantly more than she'd ever come across—and
she was *here*, as his guest. An occurrence he still
seemed less-than-thrilled about.

"You have a box?" She hazarded conversation
once again.

Stone-faced, he nodded, then gestured toward refreshments available for a coin.

"Thank you, but no," she told him, far too uncomfortably aware to eat or drink anything. She patted her hair, afraid the feathers might incinerate if his glare became any fiercer. For a man who insisted he *wanted* to be out with her, he seemed remarkably disgruntled. "I'm not thirsty, but if you—"

He grunted and took off toward the right, her light hold on his forearm whisking her down the passageway as effectively as if he'd picked her up and tossed her ahead. Practically skipping to keep up with him, she prayed the figure-filling padding would stay put. The last thing she needed was to leave a trail of dropped cotton marking her every step.

Narrow doors flanked the corridor, spaced every few feet. They passed a dozen or more before he slowed to find the one he sought. Like most, it was closed. He turned the handle and stepped back, gesturing for her to precede him.

After the well-lit hallway, it took her eyes a few seconds to adjust to the darkened interior. In that short time, she was showered with a wealth of impressions.

Smaller than she'd expected, the box itself was a cozy space, extending only a few paces in either direction. From about waist high, it opened out in the front, overlooking not only the massive stage currently occupied by twirling ballerinas—what an unexpected boon!—but the opening also allowed a glimpse into the noisy gallery below and beyond that—

Thea gasped at the magnitude of it all. Why, there had to be five levels of private boxes, all filled with an assortment of gaily dressed people. Branches of candles extended out every few boxes, illuminating some areas better than others, but everywhere her flitting glance landed, a new and dazzling sight met her eyes.

The spinning, jumping ballerinas cavorting across the stage; a full orchestra playing in front; and behind the musicians, the writhing pit of masculine voices and shapes, only half of whose attention was focused on the performers, the others—like Thea—craned their heads to inspect the individuals lining the boxes on either side.

Some of the occupants stood near the openings, gazing raptly at the stage, others conversed, paying no heed to the spectacle they'd come to see, and others...well, more than one box had the curtain pulled for complete privacy and if she wasn't mistaken—it was difficult to be certain, given the distance and amount of smoke the many candles gave off—but across the expanse, in one of the highest boxes, she *thought* she glimpsed a pair of exposed breasts just before they were covered by two broad palms and both bodies disappeared into the shadowed recess—

Thea swallowed hard and quickly returned her

attention to the private box *she* was privileged enough to enjoy tonight.

Chairs. There were several. She blinked as they came into focus.

Oh Lord, levitate me right to Lincolnshire! Lord Tremayne had barged into the wrong box—for two of the chairs were occupied.

The impressions of grandeur still brimming in her mind, one thought screamed above the others: *Escape!*

She reversed direction but he'd come up behind her, his hard body preventing retreat. His breath caught audibly as he took notice of their company.

Then everyone spoke at once.

"Tremayne?"

"*Daniel?*"

"Ellie!" burst from the man behind her, the immovable force who curved one hand around the side of her waist with a tense grip that should have hurt—but oddly didn't. "Wylde. What…"

The other man gained his feet, giving the impression of pure, lean elegance. He was immaculately turned out, not a strand of dark blond hair askew. But his lips? Those were definitely off-kilter as he shot her a contemplative look. A single look that conveyed various emotions: curiosity, speculation, censure perhaps? (And she'd thought Lord Tremayne had an intense manner?) Stepping toward them, he said, "Appears we both chose the same night."

When the woman stood and came to his side,

Thea tried again to edge around Lord Tremayne. The bite of his fingers stayed the impulse.

What should she do?

The slight blonde fixed her with a decidedly inquisitive stare.

Under ordinary circumstances, Thea was confident she could hold her own. But this was anything but ordinary. Associating with Sarah and Lord Penry and others of the demimonde ilk was one thing. But a man did *not* mingle his mistress with his—

His *what*?

Who were these people to Lord Tremayne? His friends?

Strangling the strings of her reticule so tightly it was a wonder they didn't snap, she gave a fast, modest curtsy to both the lord and his lady (as competently a curtsy as one can make when their waist is shackled). "Pardon us for the interruption," she said since no one else seemed inclined to speak since the initial outbursts. "We'll take ourselves off, let you return to your evening alone. Forgive us."

But though she again pressed into the brick wall that was Lord Tremayne, he refused to waver. And though Thea *knew* they had to leave, the scrutiny on the other couple's faces was growing.

It was as though she dreamed the next few moments when the woman stepped forward, ignoring the indrawn hiss of her companion, to offer a shallow curtsy of her own. Her eyes flicked back and forth between Thea and the man behind her. "Daniel, aren't you going to introduce me?"

DARING DECLARATIONS—Mistress in the Making, Book Three

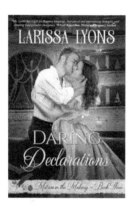

First, he showed his thoughtful generosity. Then he shared his risqué humor. Now it's time he declares everything... If only he didn't constantly wrestle with words!

An evening at the opera could prove Lord Tremayne's undoing when he and his lovely new paramour cross paths with his sister and brother-in-law. Introducing one's socially unacceptable strumpet to his stunned family is *never* done. But Daniel does it anyway. And it might just be the best decision he's ever made, for Thea's quickly become much more than a mistress—and it's time he told her so.

Thea's fallen under the enticing spell of her new protector. How could she not when his very presence, every kindness and written word has utterly seduced her senses? Yet her mind insists on knowing more, such as why must Lord Tremayne pummel his face in boxing matches and be so abrupt in person? Curiosity turns to baffled amazement when his sister seeks out Thea, begging advice. If that weren't surprising enough, when circumstances conspire and Thea arrives—unannounced—at his home, she's not only welcomed inside but confronted with more truths than she ever expected.

Mistress in the Making Trilogy

ABOUT LARISSA

A lifelong Texan, Larissa writes sexy contemporaries, spicy regencies and upbeat-ending erotica, blending heartfelt emotion with doses of laugh-out-loud humor. Her heroes are strong men with a weakness for the right woman.

When not bowing to the whims of her fluffy felines, Larissa avoids housework one word at a time. She adores brownies, James Bond and her husband—though not necessarily in that order.

Learn more by visiting LarissaLyons.com.

f facebook.com/larissa.lyons.501
o instagram.com/larissa_lyons_author
a amazon.com/author/larissalyons
BB bookbub.com/authors/larissa-lyons
g goodreads.com/larissalyons

Sparks, and stockings, fly when an interview for a husband turns into a game of forfeits—played with articles of clothing—a scandalous lady and one handsome rogue learn how very right for each other they are.

Lady Scandal **awarded the Golden Nib!** "I can't praise this book enough. Regency fans, if you like gorgeous wit in with your devilishly superb, well written, sexy reading matter, Lady Scandal should be on your 'Must Read' list." *Natalie, Miz Love & Crew Love's Books*

Top Pick from ARe Café: "[Lady Scandal] is the most flirtatious, sensual, and delectable treat." *Lady Rhyleigh, ARe Café* ~ Selected as a **Recommended Read!**

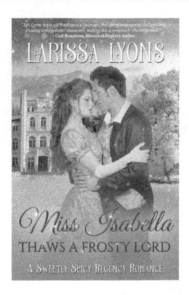

Blind from a young age, a Regency heroine risks her overbearing father's displeasure by attending a house party, never dreaming she'll meet a formidable lord who will discover all her secrets and still want her for his own.

Top Pick! "This entertaining read conjured up the atmosphere and exquisitely formal dance of manners so beloved in Jane Austen's books...I am enchanted by the grace and artful wordplay that accompanies this tale." *ELF, Night Owl Reviews*

"I love the way that the book reads as if it were written in Regency times. I'm a fan of Carla Kelly Regency romances and I was in the mood for another story of that caliber. I definitely got that with *Miss Isabella Thaws a Frosty Lord*." *EKDuncan*

Historicals by Larissa Lyons

MISTRESS IN THE MAKING series

Seductive Silence

Lusty Letters

Daring Declarations

FUN & SEXY REGENCY ROMANCE

Lady Scandal

Lady Imposter - coming soon

A SWEETLY SPICY REGENCY

Miss Isabella Thaws a Frosty Lord

———————◖◗———————

Contemporaries by Larissa Lynx

SEXY CONTEMPORARY ROMANCE

Renegade Kisses

Starlight Seduction

EROTIC ROMANCE & EROTICA

My Two-Stud Stand

Her Three Studs

Braving Donovan's

A Heart for Adam...& Rick!

No Guts, No 'Gasms

CPSIA information can be obtained
at www.ICGtesting.com
Printed in the USA
LVHW041717310820
664662LV00011B/2461

9 781949 426182